Taming the Wildcat

A Book in the Deerskin Peaks Series

Book Two

J. Raven Wilde

J. Raven Wilde

Copyright © 2021 J. Raven Wilde

All rights reserved. This book or any portion thereof may not be reproduced or used in any manner whatsoever without the express permission of the author.

This is a work of fiction. Names, places, characters, and incidents are either products of the author's imagination or used fictitiously and any resemblance to actual persons, living or dead, or businesses, organizations, or locales, is completely coincidental.

This work is intended for adult audiences only. It contains extremely sexually explicit and graphic scenes and language which may be offensive to some readers. This book is strictly intended for those over the age of 18.

Published by Twisted Crow Press, LLC.
www.twistedcrowpress.com

ISBN: 979-8-9906871-3-4

Other Books by J. Raven Wilde

Standalone Novels

His Orders

Hot and Steamy Series

In Hot Pursuit

Hot Rod

One Hot Weekend

Falling For Series

Falling for the Rancher

Falling for the Cowboy

The Mummy's Curse Mini-Series

The Mummy's Curse Vol 1

The Sorcerer's Curse Vol 2

The Curse of Anubis Vol 3

The Mummy's Curse Mini-Series Box Set

Sanctuary Series

Claimed by the Alpha

The Omega and the Witch

The Rogue and the Rebel

Deerskin Peaks Series

Claimed by the Bear

Taming the Wildcat

1

Amber

Pulling up outside the restaurant, she wanted a cigarette. She hadn't smoked in years, but dinner with her parents was always stressful, especially lately. The way they talked to her, trying to plan every aspect of her life as if she were just a passenger of her life, was annoying. They never listened to her. Well, okay so maybe not never. But they tended to discount her opinion on most everything. She wasn't a child anymore. She had dreams. She had plans.

Taking a deep breath, she tried to ready herself for the storm that was likely waiting for her inside the restaurant. The idea of a cigarette between her fingers and that sweet smoke tumbling into her lungs was almost too much to bear. She licked her lips thinking about it.

What was wrong with her?

When her dad divorced her mother, they had tried hard to get along for Amber's sake. She appreciated what they had tried to do, she really did. They were both very civil during holidays, trying to make it as normal as they could for her while growing up. It was sweet but it was a lie. They couldn't stand each other.

They had done such a good job hiding all the resentment and discord, that Amber hadn't picked up on it until she was almost ten and caught them fighting behind closed doors only to come out later acting as if nothing happened. Thinking about it now, she realized both of her parents were excellent liars. That didn't instill a lot of confidence in her, knowing she was about to go in and have dinner with them, along with her stepmom, Tammy. At least dinner with them was only once every other week.

Over the years, her mother had slowly distanced herself from her father and his new life and in the process had inadvertently pushed Amber away too. It made her sad in a way she had never thought possible. Amber did her best to reach out with cards and texts, but they weren't always answered and she'd kind of given up on trying to have the kind of relationship she'd wanted with her mother. So, Amber wouldn't be surprised if she didn't show up. She rarely did unless it was to set her up on a date with someone.

At least Tammy hadn't tried to insert herself as a surrogate mom. In that respect, Amber had to kind of hand it to her. If in her shoes, Amber wasn't sure she could've handled it the same way. On occasion, Tammy had tried to insert herself as a matchmaker, it would stand to reason she'd want to take over every aspect of her life but she hadn't. It gave her pause, considering what it might mean. Maybe Amber was more of a lost cause than she'd thought. There's a confidence builder. Just what she needed heading into the gauntlet.

Whenever they all got together there were constant eye rolls and snarky comments left and right. It was exhausting being around them. She felt like she'd participated in one of those Iron Man Triathlons. Always exhausted, angry, and filled with just a pinch of resentment that she didn't come out winning in the end. It wasn't that she didn't love them, because she did. It was more they drove her insane trying to manage every aspect of her life. She figured, she'd made it this far without causing too much damage, how hard could the rest of her life's journey be? She was tired of always having her life managed. Amber felt like she wasn't in control of anything. Her dad and Tammy thought she still wasn't ready to adult just yet.

Thus, the desire to smoke.

Sitting in her car, music trying to blare her soul clean, she took a deep breath. She always came with some made-up information to confuse her dad and Tammy so they wouldn't zero in on a single aspect of her life to try and better it. She'd learned the trick from her brother William. Ah, sweet William.

Now there was another type of annoyance. He was a sweetheart. A smile flickered on her lips thinking about him.

It quickly left thought about what the purpose of tonight was about, realizing her dad and Tammy would likely want to talk about setting her up with someone. That was always part of the litany of these get-togethers. Why couldn't they get it through their heads? She wasn't interested in settling down with anyone. She wanted to have fun. It was no secret to her close friends, that Amber loved sex and loved sleeping with different men. She used a bunch of different dating apps to satisfy her needs. None of them were designed to find husbands and life partners. She was clear in what she wanted but her dad had other ideas.

If her dad had his way, she'd be married within the year. That was his goal. She knew it was. Get her married off and pregnant so he doesn't have to worry about her anymore. Okay, so maybe that was a little harsh, but it's how he made her feel when he talked about the men he wanted to set her up with. It was like he had some internal checklist that made these men good candidates. None of them were attractive or interesting to her. None of them ever turned her on. Her legs were never weakened, she never had that little skip in her heart, and they never tried to swoon her the right way. She didn't get that lovely little tingle between her legs after being with any of them.

For her dad, it was less about the men turning his daughter on and more about making sure she was taken care of financially like she wasn't able to work and earn her own money. It was never a former college athlete with wide shoulders, a muscular build, and a thick cock. No, sir. Tammy and her dad always picked the accountant's son from where her dad worked ten years ago or the bartender's kid from where her mother liked to drown her sorrows. It was annoying and never someone with allure or promise, or that wicked glint in their eye that let her know they wanted to bend her over the hood of the car and lift her skirt. Just thinking about that, made her tingle.

At least William would be there. As far as little brothers go, he was all right. He wasn't like a normal little brother. She knew all little brothers were annoying to one degree or another but hers took it to a new level. She'd thought he might outgrow it at some point but no luck so far. That's not to say they weren't close because they were. They were closer than most of her friends were with their siblings. William had trusted her enough to come out to her about his sexuality years before coming out to anyone else. It had meant so much to her that he had done that, trusted her with something so personal. She'd confided in him about how sexual she was and how she didn't want to settle down. He'd even helped her pick out a few guys to bed. She loved him for accepting her as she was. She just wished her parents would do the same.

Why was she even coming to this dinner? It was going to be a shit show. She knew it. And yet, here she was ten minutes early—because who wanted to show up late to your own execution—fingers nervously tapping on the steering wheel, wishing there was a pack of cigarettes in the glove box. There weren't any. She'd checked twice. She was being ridiculous.

Flipping down the sun visor, she checked out how she looked in the mirror. Amber thought the tiny lights on either side of the mirror always made her face look jaundiced. That being said, she looked damn fine. Too bad it was going to be wasted on a dinner with her parents. She took a deep breath and held it, counting to ten slowly before letting it go. Rubbing fingers beneath her eyes, and teasing her dark hair just a bit more, she decided it was time to go. No better time than the present to be ripped to shreds by your parents while sharing dinner.

It was worse than bringing home a date for the first time to meet them. She wondered who they'd try to fix her up with this time. They'd gone through the majority of the single guys she knew and started to take recommendations from their friends. How sad was that? Not only did her dad and stepmom think she couldn't find a suitable man to date but they had sent out the alert to all of their friends as well.

Amber shouldn't have been surprised. The last few times she'd gone over to visit her mother, Mrs. Galugli, the pack's matchmaker, had come over to 'talk' which meant to talk to her about her son or her son's friend or her son's friend's cousin. Pretty soon it was going to be with the guy she randomly saw at the gas station who seemed to have a good smile.

It was bad enough her parents didn't think she was capable of finding a date but now to have the entire neighborhood in her business was a little too much. It was part of living in a small town where everybody knew everybody and there was nothing better than a juicy bit of gossip to share. Amber wasn't like that but she knew everyone else was.

Taking the keys out of the ignition, because she couldn't stand the humiliation of having to be driven home by her dad to get her spare set of keys for a second time, she put them in her small clutch and got out of the car. She smoothed down her skirt, loving the cut just above the knee, and checked the strap around the back of her ankle. She liked the dress, but the heels were the clincher. They accented her calves and boosted her confidence weirdly. It wasn't anything she could put her finger on. It wasn't like her at all but she did like to get dressed up now and then.

Walking across the street, she smiled at the dark-haired man waiting to cross the street who was checking her out. He waved, so she answered it one of her own, and then disaster struck. She caught her toe on the edge of the curb and almost fell, twisting her other ankle in the process. Only by the slimmest of margins was she able to catch herself before sprawling on the sidewalk armed with skinned knees and disaster.

For a moment, she looked like an awkward crane, her legs wobbly, arms outstretched. Two boys on the nearby bench chuckled. She wanted to introduce them to a fist but chose to just offer them her middle finger instead. They laughed harder. The man who had been watching her was long gone. Who could blame him? Nobody wants to blame someone who could cause physical injury simply by crossing the street.

Looking down at her shoes, she frowned, realizing she'd scuffed the toe. She'd just gotten them last weekend. This was simply perfect. If her mind wasn't cluttered with anxious thoughts, she wouldn't have tripped over her own feet.

She'd have to dig out the right colored marker to color in the scuff mark. The rest of the shoe still looked great. No sense in throwing them out over one scuff mark. That was something her mother would've said. She hated she was becoming more like her every single day.

Having picked up her dignity from the sidewalk, she climbed the four steps to the front door of the restaurant and didn't hesitate to walk inside. She spotted her mother waving to her from the other side of the restaurant, the little seed of worry beginning to bloom even further. Amber couldn't stand that her parents made her this nervous. She silently wished that she didn't show. Now it was going to be three against one.

Making her way to the table, she weaved past the salad bar and took her seat, both her mother and dad beaming. Her stepmom, Tammy was busy eyeing the waiter, holding her empty martini glass up in the air. Amber wondered how many glasses she had consumed already.

"Well, don't you look absolutely stunning." Her dad smiled while he remained standing until she took her seat. He was undeniably old school, cordial, polite, with a touch of chivalry. His hair was grayer and his face more wrinkled. His eyes were still bright and the voice strong, but he was aging faster than she'd ever thought possible and she was sure it was either from his job or from being married to her stepmother while still dealing with his ex-wife.

"Agreed. What a beautiful dress," her mother added, clasping her hands beneath her chin looking her up and down, smiling appreciatively. Unlike her Dad, her mother, on the other hand, fought aging like a dying Valkyrie from Asgard, forever battling every wrinkle, every gray hair. Amber was fairly sure she was singlehandedly keeping the hair coloring business afloat. And the perfume company. And the jewelers. And the clothing designers.

How was she not exhausted from putting in that much effort to appear flawless? Amber was ready for a nap and had only put in the effort for a few hours to ready herself not a lifetime like her mother.

"Thanks. How is everybody?" Taking her seat, she could feel the tension. She wondered if something had been said that started a fight. It wouldn't be the first time.

"Great." William seemed thrilled to be there as always. He was slouched down, looking like some nine-year-old kid who was bored rather than someone who was twenty-two. He leaked immaturity with every word he spoke and every eye roll. It didn't matter though. She still loved him. As much as they bickered, they got along well.

"So glad to see you too, darling brother."

He stuck out his tongue at her playfully.

"We took the liberty of ordering you a water with lemon." Her father said it like he had just saved the President from a batch of bad alcohol, but she was going to need some wine. Her father would frown on her if she drank a beer. The common streetwalkers drank beer. She had always wanted to ask her dad how many streetwalkers he had polled before coming to that conclusion but figured she'd save that for another day.

"Thanks." She wished she'd thought to bring a travel bottle of whiskey.

"Why are you dressed like a hooker?" her brother whispered loudly.

"How do you know what a hooker looks like?" she scoffed at William. They always played games, teasing each other.

"Because my sister looks like one. Have you met her?" he said, giving her a wink.

She was tempted to playfully toss her napkin at him but held back on account her parents would make a fuss, but she didn't have to wait long.

"Both of you stop it," her mother snapped. She didn't even look at them as she was too immersed in her phone, a flicker of a smile teasing her lips for a heartbeat or two. It was probably whatever wonderful stud she'd found perched on a stool down at the bar.

"Can we just have a civil dinner?" her dad sighed as he spread his napkin across his lap. The waiter brought Amber a water with lemon, along with her stepmom's martini.

"Excuse me. Can you bring me a white wine too, please?" Amber said with her head held high.

Her mother put her phone down and her dad put his glass back on the table, William hid his laughter behind his hand. All three of them stared at her, her parent's faces like pale dinner plates, frozen, unmoving.

"Why aren't you having water with lemon?" Her dad was eyeing her like a scientist watching his test subject react in the exact opposite way as predicted.

"I am," Amber shrugged as she took a deliberate drink and placed the glass down. "I'm also having white wine. I'm twenty-five. Not like I'm breaking any human or pack law. I'm an adult."

Her dad was about to say something when her mother put her hand across his arm. It was the first physical contact she'd ever witnessed since the divorce. "You're allowed to have wine. It's just … odd, that's all."

"Odd that I'm making decisions for myself and acting like an adult for once?"

"That's not what I meant," her mother replied and then there was an odd silence that stretched for a moment, her mother batting her eyes a bit too many times before splaying her hands out on either side of her plate. It was one of her mother's tells.

Oh, goody. Let the games begin. Amber sighed.

"I met someone the other day. A young man from this pack down south. He was up here visiting relatives. Has a great smile and seems so very sweet. Oh, and he's very handsome."

"I'm so happy for you, mother. I wish you both the best," Amber replied, sipping her lemon water again.

Her mother scoffed and then snorted as she laughed. "Oh, you're too much."

William remained with his face stuck in his phone, not even bothering to look up or chime in to save his sister. He stopped helping ages ago when it appeared as if he was going to be next in their parent's mate arrangement.

"He's not for me. I meant for you to date him."

"Oh, so you wanted to try him out first, mother? How very forward-thinking of you."

Her mother turned red, mouth hanging open. "Amber, please."

Her dad turned to her; eyes hard as if to say Amber had crossed a line.

Amber glanced over at Tammy, curious why she hadn't spoken up yet. Maybe she was waiting for her chance to add in her two cents. Amber had to speak her peace before she did.

"Let me save you all the trouble. I'm sure you have your lists of men you'd like to set me up with but I'm already dating someone.

The white wine came just in the nick of time. She didn't let it breathe. She didn't smell it first. She took two quick swallows, the flavor exploding across her tongue.

Her mother and dad just stared at her and then looked at each other, her dad shifting in his seat, elbows now on the table.

Tammy sipped her martini quietly before saying, "You are?"

Amber nodded.

"I call BS. No way." Her stepmom put her hand on William's arm. "What?"

Tammy frowned at William, she turned to Amber and asked, "Who is this guy you're dating?"

Amber scoffed, a light chuckle following. "Not a chance." She wasn't telling anyone who it was as they would have him pulled up on their phones and psycho-analyze him before she could finish her wine.

Her dad cleared his throat and tried to smile but it looked more like a grimace. "How long have you been seeing him?"

Amber shrugged, trying to look relaxed but feeling anything but, her insides grumbling. "Maybe two months."

"Maybe? She's making it up." William winked at her and balled up his napkin, tossing it on the table.

"No, I'm not."

She wasn't dating the guy. It was someone she liked on a dating app. They'd been hooking up for the last month and the sex was good enough to keep her coming back for more. But not good to keep her from sleeping with other guys she met on there. He'd hinted at wanting to spend the night and do other 'date' like things, but she wasn't interested. She wanted to experience everything life had to offer. She didn't want to be tied down to anyone. Not yet. Now tied down by anyone? That's a different story. She smiled.

"When can we meet him?" Her mother was trying to look innocent but it wasn't working. Her horns were showing.

"Oh, please. Not happening."

She finished her wine, frowning. Were the glasses getting smaller?

"Amber, we're worried about you." Her dad was back to looking more like himself, his eyes didn't appear like hard shards anymore.

"I'm fine, Dad." She tried to dismiss him but it was hard. They'd been so close while she was growing up but things had changed since the divorce. It wasn't that they weren't close anymore, it's just that it was a different kind of close. She missed her dad, and the way things used to be.

"Is this guy even someone from the pack?" her dad asked softly, concern in his tone.

"What difference does it make, Dad? I'm not marrying him. I'm just—" She caught herself when she said the word, but it didn't matter. Her meaning was clear, she didn't want to marry anyone yet.

"Are you sure that's a good idea?" her mother asked.

"What? Is what a good idea? That I'm having sex, mother? That I'm enjoying myself and experiencing things? Is that what you're worried about." Amber realized she was being too loud. Customers at nearby tables turned to look at them.

"Amber." Her mother adopted her admonishing tone, her father taking a deep breath.

Why had she worn this dress and done her makeup? This was such a waste of time. She should've known it would turn out to be a mess. Who was she trying to impress? Her brother had summed it up. Her whole family thought she was dressed like a whore. She knew she looked great. Sexy. Hot. The whole nine. But it seemed like the effort was wasted.

She was about to call the waiter for another glass of wine when her phone rang. It was Misty her best friend.

"Is it your new guy?" Tammy asked with a raised brow.

Scoffing, Amber shook her head. "It's Misty."

"Tell her we said, 'hi'," her stepmom said, smiling like everything was just peaches and cream.

"Hello?"

"Hey, Amber."

Amber could tell something was wrong right away. Misty's voice didn't sound like her at all.

"What's wrong?"

The sobs were frightening. Misty never cried like this. If she had to guess, she'd say it had something to do with Lyle. He was a member of Amber's pack and was nothing but bad news. She'd tried to warn Misty about him but it didn't do any good. In the end, Amber figured Misty would just have to figure it out on her own. She was slowly starting to realize he was a piece of crap. He'd cheated on her at least once and probably more than that. He was a horndog if there ever was one.

"Tell her we said 'hi'." Amber ignored her stepmom, wondering if Lyle had gotten physical with Misty. Was that why she sounded so strange?

Her parents had accepted Misty as much as they could, given she was a human. While they claimed it didn't bother them, Amber knew it did on some level. They knew about her hard-luck story and knew what a great influence she was on their daughter's life.

"Okay. I'll be right there." Disconnecting the call, Amber stood up.

"Wait. What are you doing?" her mother asked.

"I'm leaving. Something's happened with Misty. She's freaking out and I need to get over there for her."

"This conversation isn't—"

"Put a sock in it, mother. I have to go." Her mother reacted as if Amber had thrown hot oil in her face.

Amber gathered up her things and headed to the door, kissing her dad on the cheek as she left.

*****

She didn't remember how she got to Misty's, her mind filling with all sorts of terrible things that she would find when she got there. Would Misty have bruises? A big black eye? Instead, she found Misty on the side of the road waiting for her. Why wasn't she inside? She noticed the overnight bag on the curb beside her. Pulling her midnight blue Mustang to the curb, she lowered the passenger window.

"Need a lift, stranger?"

"How'd ya know?" Misty offered a small smile, but it didn't last.

"Get in. Let's blow this town."

They drove for a few minutes in silence, the music so low on Amber's radio, that Misty couldn't tell what song was playing. Thankfully, Amber broke the odd silence.

"You need to get away from him. Far, *far* away." Amber says. "Leave the sucker for good. You've been naive enough to stay with him after he cheated the first time. You'd be a damn fool to stick around now."

"You're right. But where would I go? My lease is up soon and I don't have another place to stay."

"I'd let you crash with me, but I have a better place in mind." Amber smiled, a sly look on her face. "My dad has a cabin in Wyoming. Real quaint. Out in the mountains with woods all around. He used to go up there for hunting, but he hasn't made the trip in years. I can loan you a car and you can take a little vacation for a few weeks. You need it after tonight."

"I don't know," Misty hesitated. She was never this impulsive "Do you think running away is a good idea?"

"You're not running away! You're taking a break from all the stress. All the Lyle BS that's built up over this year. It's a break and a well-deserved break at that."

"Fine," Misty finally agreed. "Maybe you're right. Maybe this will be good for me. I've always wanted to go camping, you know."

"It's not really camping. It's a cabin with water, electricity, and a roof. It's not like I'm giving some ratty old tent and a compass."

They laughed together. Amber was always good to her.

"Fine. I'll go."

"Perfect!" Amber did a quick happy clap. "This is a fresh start for you as a single woman, Misty. Now that you're back on the market, Wyoming better watch out!"

2

Jack

His heart wasn't in it today. He could just tell. For the first time in a long time, it felt like work. And that wasn't a good thing. When it became work, that meant his mind wandered and he lost his focus. Losing focus when you were dangling hundreds of feet up from a woven bit of nylon could be deadly.

Jack loved climbing, absolutely loved it, but for some reason, today, it just wasn't happening. He wasn't feeling the rush he always felt working his way up the rock face of the mountains around his home. Once that rush passed, he always had an overwhelming sense of calm. Relaxing even with all the physical activity necessary to complete the climb. Nothing was pulling him out of his funk.

What was going on with him?

His best friend, Tate, was climbing with him today. He was the sheriff of the little mountain town he called home. They'd known each other for more than half of his life which was a little unsettling to say. It gave him pause to think about how much of his life had already passed.

He and Tate lived in the same town, Deerskin Peaks. It was a small town neatly wedged into the small, surrounding mountain range.

"What's your problem today?"

He avoided Tate's gaze. How was he supposed to answer his friend when he had no idea what the answer was?

He shrugged, the two of them readying their ropes for the descent down the opposite face of the mountain they'd just climbed over the course of three hours. They both liked the hard work it took to climb the step peaks around the town. Usually, he welcomed the hard work. It was always typically worth it by way of the views they found. Some of the most beautiful sunsets exploded around the mountain peaks. They were second to none, but today he could take it or leave it.

"What?" Jack asked as he caught Tate staring at him for a moment.

"That," Tate pointed at him. "I'm talking about that right here. You're distracted. Where's your head at, because it sure as hell isn't here. What's wrong with you?"

Jack shrugged, "I don't know, man. I'm just out of it, I guess."

"We didn't need to do this today if you weren't up for it."

Jack coughed, clearing his throat. "No, I'm good. I mean we've been planning this climb for a week now."

"Yeah, we have."

"So, that's why I'm here." Jack said as he stared at his climbing rope.

"Such a good soldier. Always reporting for friend duty."

"Screw you," Jack said jokingly.

"No, thanks. I'm not that kind of friend."

"Thank God," Jack laughed. "If I had to look at your hairy ass every morning, I'd hang myself in the shower."

"Such a cliché. I knew you were staring at my ass."

"Shut up. I don't really."

"You just admitted to it," Tate joked.

They both chuckled, still working on getting their lines ready as a nice breeze kicked up, cooling them off.

"You need to make sure you're focused heading back down, okay?"

"Okay, Dad," Jack chuckled.

"Look, seriously. Not being focused and aware is not a good state of mind while climbing a mountain." Tate crossed his eyes at him, making his best friend smile.

"Okay, okay. You make a good point."

The clouds were in rare form today. They looked like little brush strokes from an artist's paintbrush — wispy bits of white against a cobalt blue sky.

"Want to get some drinks after we're done here?" Tate asked sniffing loudly.

Why anyone with allergies like his would choose to live out in the wilds was beyond him, but that's what the fool was doing. Tate was the first bear shifter Jack knew that had allergies.

"I don't know. I guess we could. But I don't know, man. I got thrown out of there last weekend."

"Little sad when the owner of the bar throws himself out of said bar."

Jack chuckled, "If that ain't the truth. Kinda like kicking your own ass."

"Only with alcohol."

"Yes, alcohol. The sweet, glorious, nectar of the gods."

Jack bought the bar right after he had gotten out of the Army and had changed it into a bar and grill which seemed to go over better with the town. It was successful enough to garner the attention of a few investors who wanted to take him to the next level by franchising it. Jack wasn't that interested. He made more than enough money off the bar and grilled to support himself comfortably and that's all that mattered. He wasn't looking for fame and fortune. The size of the headaches would be monumental trying to manage that kind of mess.

No thanks.

The messes he had to manage now owning a single restaurant were big enough for his liking. Thank you very much.

Jack and Tate had served together in the Army. Tate was like a brother to him considering he was a werepanther and Tate a bear shifter. Tate had re-upped his papers and stayed another four years after Jack checked out. The bar did more than okay. It was the only bar and grill in town. And, considering it solely relied on the town of Deerskin Peaks which was a tiny town by anyone's measure Jack was more than happy with the money he made.

Jack's werepanther pack lived in the thick forests in the area surrounding Deerskin Peaks. When Tate got out of the Army, he came to Deerskin Peaks and became sheriff. They hadn't planned on living in the same town once they got out of the Army. It wasn't even a conversation they'd had. Sure, they'd talked about staying in touch, but not to this degree. It was weird how things worked out sometimes, but Jack was glad for it. He enjoyed Tate's friendship.

The sunset was reaching for them, the inkwells of the sky opening up spilling color over everything in its path, tinting the wispy brushstrokes of clouds. He had never known beauty to this level. Jack had never thought about the world around him, at least not the natural world as beautiful. He'd never truly been drawn to nature. But after moving back to this town and seeing it firsthand as a military veteran, he was a fan for life.

Things had always gone by so fast with him before moving back to Deerskin Peaks. Now, he was able to take a deep breath and just connect with the world around him. It kept him calm. It kept him centered.

They both sat down for a minute before getting ready to head back down. Drinking some bottled water, they watched the colors as they marched into the fading daylight, staining the darkness with their beautiful hues.

"So, were you serious about what you'd said earlier?" Tate asked.

"Yes, I have slept with six pairs of identical twins. At the same time."

Tate just stared at him with raised eyebrows. He tugged on his gloves, getting ready for the descent. "There's something seriously wrong with you. Not to mention your eyes are turning brown because you're so full of it."

They laughed together before Jack cleared his throat. "Look, I'm serious about trying to find someone to settle down with. I don't want to go through life single and die some old bachelor everyone feels sorry for that is holed up in some miserly estate."

"Miserly estate? Really? Where is the money going to come from to support that fantasy?" Tate joked and Jack couldn't help but grin.

"I figured, I would murder a few local business owners and take over their establishments and rake in the dough. Hopefully, the sheriff will look the other way."

"Wow, that kind of sounds like you're a wannabe mobster. It doesn't support your miserly estate fantasy. For me, that sounds like you need to be a Scrooge."

Jack smiled, chuckling. "I guess it kind of does."

"Are you serious about settling down?" They always joked with each other even when talking about serious stuff. They always had and always would. It was just the way they acted around each other.

Nodding, Tate took a deep breath before saying, "Yeah. I think I'd like to get married in the next couple of years. I mean, I'm not getting any younger."

"True and you're getting uglier too." Jack punched his friend in the arm, laughing "I mean I'm thirty-five, man. I'm fast approaching that weirdness plane. I'm starting to get those creepy looks if I'm in a park by myself. I'm turning into a creeper."

Tate tossed a rock and hit a nearby tree. "You're not a creeper."

"No, not yet. But I'm fast approaching creeper status."

Tate tossed another one but missed this time. "What does creeper status even mean?"

Jack shrugged, downing the rest of his water. "I'm not sure, but when and if I get there, I'll let you know."

"Oh, good, a learning experience. You always take such good care of me, brother."

They both stood and headed over to the brim, looking down the length of the mountain they had climbed. It was impressive. The sad thing was he'd been in no state of mind to enjoy it. He wondered if it had to do with what Tate had talked about. Finding a mate. Not wanting to be alone. It was certainly time for them to both find someone, but Tate had already beat him to it and Jack was happy for him, but now, it was his turn.

"So, what are you going to do about it? The creeper status, I mean. When you get there," Tate asked as he prepared to descend.

It was a good question; one he had been thinking about more than at any other point in his life. He was thinking about kids and raising a family. It was tugging on Jack's heart in a way nothing ever had before.

"I don't know. I hadn't thought about it. The women I've gone out with from town have been okay but not okay enough to warrant taking a dip in the gene pool with them. There hasn't been one I could picture myself with for the rest of my life."

"I get it. I was the same way until I met Misty. I wasn't looking for anything either."

"That's what my Mom used to say that love usually happened. When you were least expecting it, boom, there it was right there in front of you."

"I used to think that was all romance novel crap but I have to admit. I'm buying into it more and more."

"Oh, so you do read romance novels," Jack poked.

"What and you don't?" Tate stared at him with raised eyebrows.

He hadn't put much stock in love-at-first-sight kind of tales either. They all seemed so contrived. Was there someone out there for everyone? He supposed so. What would it take to meet his life partner? Would he even recognize her for what she was? He hoped so.

Jack had never strongly considered getting married. Yes, when given the time, Jack liked to think about having kids. The idea of watching his children grow up and succeed was something he wanted. He was just busy with other things like taking over his father's role in the family and running the bar. Maybe it was time to start considering it. Settling down. Family. Kids.

His inner panther mewed at the thought. He was the alpha of his pack. It was time he added onto it and started a family.

3

Amber

Dating apps were always hit or miss for her. Not their functionality. I mean they all operated under the same premise. You look through pictures and pick someone who doesn't make you want to throw up. You contact them, hook up and that's it. The problem was not every picture matched the person who showed up for the date. Now, for her, it wasn't always a big deal. She wasn't looking for Mr. Right. She was looking for Mr. Right Now. Looks, money, station, all those things were less important to her. Hell, she just wanted a warm body who wasn't a prude in bed that would give her what she ached for and then move on down the road.

Now, the times when the picture had either been photoshopped beyond recognition or was clearly from a decade ago were some of the most fun for her. It made the date interesting. She made a game of it. Watching a guy tap dancing trying to explain that his sister uploaded an older picture of him as a joke and he couldn't figure out how to replace it was always fun. Explaining why they were forty pounds heavier than the picture they used was fun too.

Guys were so transparent.

Waiting in the restaurant, she'd already had two wines. She was nervous and she didn't know why. Amber was anything but nervous when it came to interacting with people. She was confident and to the point. Amber didn't do anything Amber didn't want to do. But, something was worrying her. Something wiggling its way through her heart. Maybe the thing with Misty had her more shaken than she wanted to admit or maybe she was just horny.

She'd go with horny.

She liked the feel of the thong, the way it caressed her, the way it felt darkly sexy when she sat down and it grew tighter between her legs. That sweet pressure against that spot at the apex of her thighs, the silky-smooth material that rubbed against her just right when she moved had Amber feeling aroused. She needed sex and needed it now.

God, let this one be hot.

Bingo.

When he walked in, his tanned face framed perfectly with dark hair, she crossed her legs letting that sweet little pressure build like it always did when she couldn't touch herself but wanted to get off. He had wide shoulders, a muscular build, and dimples when he smiled. He waved to her and she waved back. He moved with confidence; his stride sure as he cut through the tables. At least this one, the picture matched the man. Thank God.

She smiled, doing her best to seem alluring. This was going to be so good. She took another sip of wine as she watched him make his way toward her, moving like a running back cutting through the line.

Coming up to the table she had been sitting at for the past fifteen minutes, he smiled and extended his hand. His nails were manicured but that wasn't what made her breath catch in her throat. No, it was the size of his hands. Thick fingers, she could very easily see around her throat, pinning her arms down, sweeping over her body, dipping inside her tight channel. She could only hope the size he was advertising with his hands would match the size of his tool below the belt.

He said enthusiastically, "So glad you reached out."

"So glad you came." She emphasized the word came, but he didn't pick up on the innuendo.

"What are you having?"

She wanted to say, "You." But didn't. Biting her tongue and squeezing her legs together so tightly, she shivered, she said, "Chablis."

His name was Rick something or other. She didn't bother with last names on the dating apps. It never mattered to her. Amber used them and then moved on. In some cases, she wished she didn't even have to learn their first names. She wasn't there for social commentary, just a warm body. Amber had no interest in their politics and associated brilliance with whatever they thought would get them into her pants. There was no doubt they would. Sometimes, it didn't happen because something about the guy turned her off, but that was rare.

If there was a way to have anonymous sex without knowing anyone's names, she would totally be down for it. It was such a turn on to not know who was stuffing her with their thickness taking her—

She realized Rick had said something and she hadn't caught in, lost in her wicked daydream.

Crap.

"I'm sorry. What?" she gave him an innocent smile.

He sat down letting go of her hand. "I just asked if you wanted another one."

Shrugging, blushing just a bit, after getting caught daydreaming, she wondered what he'd think if he felt how wet she was. Would he bypass all the bullshit and just take her home now? That sent another little wave of pleasure down between her legs but she behaved, saying, "Sure."

After two Chablis for her and three beers for him, she was feeling that lovely fuzziness around everything. She could tell she was giggling a lot but didn't care. Rick was yummy looking and she couldn't wait to have a taste. She didn't even care if he was human.

"I work in IT. Do a little developing on the side but mostly tech support. Not a dream job but it pays the bills."

She knew what he meant. Amber hadn't found her dream job yet but knew it wasn't as an accountant working at her father's law office. She'd thought working with the law would be rewarding and exciting. Saving the innocent and all that. What she found out was the law sucked. It was boring and the seven years she'd worked there she'd only been to court once. Everything was settled with plea bargains and back door meetings.

"Computers? That's pretty cool." She frowned. Why was she suddenly feeling like she was back in ninth grade talking to Jerry Phillips, the starting quarterback? His locker had been right above hers and he would sometimes talk to her. She sometimes liked to think about going to prom with him but he was going out with Sharon Zemeckis and it seemed pretty serious.

"Not a lot of cool stuff happens really. Just me and a screen pounding out keystrokes. That's it."

Nodding, she realized the conversation was dying and so was her chances of getting laid. Even though he said he worked on computers, he didn't look like a typical nerd. No pocket protector. No tape on his glasses. Hell, no glasses at all. He didn't say things like hard drive or RAM or anything like that.

Though she'd love for him to ram her. Was she not sending the right signals? Maybe she'd had one drink too many.

"Well, it sounds way more exciting than my job."

"What do you do?"

"Accountant for a law firm." She figured she'd leave out the part it was her father's law firm. That was usually a buzzkill. After all, she didn't want him to think that she was still daddy's girl. She paid her bills and had lived on her own for almost five years now. Never mind that it was in the guest house in the back of her parents' house.

"Numbers."

Nodding, she said, "Numbers."

This was turning bad quick. Not even the thong was helping anymore.

"What do you like to do for fun?" he asked.

"Hey, Amber."

She turned to see another of her conquests walking toward her. Oh, no.

"Why haven't you called me back?" Running his fingers through his hair a few times quickly, he crossed his arms and then tucked his hands in his back pockets. He was so mad he couldn't seem to figure out what to do with his hands. It was kind of comical.

"Just not that interested, Brad."

"That's not the impression I got." The guy had been so full of himself he barely paid attention to her in the bedroom. He was too interested in getting himself off he completely forgot about her.

"Well, it's not hard to get the wrong impression when you have a dick the size of my pinky and you didn't bother helping me achieve my own orgasm instead of worrying about your own."

Two guys at the table next to them laughed, and a woman on the other side of them turned to stare.

"You're in for the ride of your life with this one," Brad said, smiling with disgust while pointing at her. When Rick didn't say anything, Brad continued, "As long as you don't mind you're nowhere near her first, she'll do you, man."

"Disgusting, Brad." She looked at her nails trying to seem as bored as she could so he'd take the hint.

"No, that's not what you said when you swal—"

Rick stood up, almost knocking over his chair in the process. He towered over Brad who seemed even more nervous now. "Think you better get going."

Brad nodded, a wild look in his eyes. "Not worth it, man. You're just the flavor of the week or whenever she wants a lick. Don't get so worked up about it. If I were you. I'd lick it, stick it, and forget it, man." Brad's smile didn't last long as it turned into a sneer. "Just another whore in my book."

Rick's punch came in high and to the right. Brad hadn't been expecting it, not that he could've done anything about it. It didn't look like Brad had been in many fights during his lifetime. He crumpled without throwing back a single punch. Amber's mouth was open and her eyes wide with shock. She couldn't believe anyone would throw a punch for her.

Too bad he was human, she would love to spend a little more time getting to know him.

They looked at each other, Rick's face stern, his eyes hard before they softened seeing her smile. They both chuckled as Brad stumbled out of the bar.

"Could we finish our date at your place?" Amber said cheerfully.

"I think that could be arranged." Rick helped her out of her chair and they headed for the door.

*****

His place was decent enough. It was clearly in need of a woman's touch but it wasn't as bad as some of the other places she'd been with a fuck buddy. She wasn't there for the aesthetics anyway. She was there for him and for what he had in his pants. Amber had been rubbing him through his pants all the way home and although muscular builds didn't always translate to big cocks, she was pleasantly surprised to what she had been palming.

He had poured some wine for them, but she never even tasted it. The blur of what she'd already had to drink was withering her willpower and her brainpower.

She was done being coy. Stepping toward him, she took off her shirt and reached behind her to undo her bra. She loved the slight chill in the air, nipples hard, body thrumming with what was to come next.

"Damn," his eyes went wide with surprise as he stared at her breasts.

She smiled. That's the reaction she wanted. She wanted him, craved him. Needed him.

They kissed, her mouth opening to his. There was no tentativeness, no awkward moments. It was just passion, desire spilling over. Her hands unzipped his pants, her hands full of his throbbing member. He felt so good. So thick.

He moaned, his hands at her breasts, his fingers tipped with hot coals as they traced lines across her bare skin. His mouth found her throat, his tongue teasing her skin, a lovely chill racing down her body as she stroked him. He moaned against the well of her throat, whiskers tempting her skin.

Hands moving up and down his shaft, he moaned against her bare breast, his mouth finding her nipple, tongue teasing it. Her body pressed against his, one of his hands moving between her legs, rubbing her through the silky fabric, God, she wanted to feel his touch against her bare skin.

She took a step away, his breathing rapid, a devious smile on his face. Turning away from him, she let him see the thong she was wearing, his eyes tracing its line, his cock hard.

"Baby, you look so good."

Slipping out of her thong, her body bare and wanton before him, she got down on her knees and took him in her mouth. She loved the first taste of his precum, feeling his erection twitch in her mouth, his body arching into her, forcing himself deeper. Flicking the underside with her tongue, she nibbled just a bit along the shaft and he jumped, moaning loudly. Letting him go, she smiled and asked, "Like that?"

"God, yes."

She pushed him back on his bed, her body alive with desire, fingertips tingling with it. Straddling him, she took every inch inside, rocking back and forth with her hips, her hair tumbling across her face, she let out a contended sigh. Rocking her hips, she let him slip in and out of her tightness as they found a rhythm, a wicked smile crossing his lips.

Rick's hands were at her hips and then slid up to her breasts, the two of them finding their rhythm, urging each other on, aching for release, their pace increasing.

"Baby," he moaned.

She rode him harder, breasts moving with the motion, his hands squeezing her soft globes harder. It wouldn't be long now.

Amber could feel her arousal building, a beautiful crescendo toward the waiting gush of desire.

With every flex of her hips, he slid in and out of her, their pace quickening, their passion consuming.

"Please fill me up," she purred.

"Yes." His voice was breathy, lust filled.

"Please. Please. Now."

As they bucked together, his hands around her lower back drawing her down on him harder, she felt that sweet build of pleasure growing between her legs, her body shivering with those waves, those beautiful waves.

She came hard and as she did, Amber felt him swell as he gushed inside her. His body arched, his member still twitching, those lovely spasms continuing for quite a while.

They stayed coupled a few moments longer before she laid down next to him, the sweet afterglow taking them both, his warmth comforting her. As he readjusted how he was lying, he reached his arm around her waist drawing her closer.

That was her signal.

It was time to go.

She didn't want him to get the wrong idea. She was here for one reason and one reason only.

His cock.

She sat up and started getting dressed.

"What's wrong?" he asked as he watched her leave the bed.

"Nothing's wrong," she replied, gathering her clothes.

She knew the questions that were coming and had her answers ready for each one. This scene had played out dozens of times over the last year.

"Then why are you going so soon?"

"I just have to make it an early night."

"Why?"

Finding her shoes and sitting on the edge of the bed, she said, "Look, this was fun and all but I have to get home and get some sleep."

She hoped she didn't sound too bitchy but in the end, she didn't care. It wasn't like she was taking Rick home to meet her parents or anything.

"So, what Brad said back at the restaurant?" his tone sounded deeper.

Hearing Brad's name was like a pinprick to her heart.

"What about it?" she replied sharply, avoiding eye contact.

"Did you really sleep with all those guys?"

She sighed, "Yeah, why?"

"That's such a turn-on."

Amber turned her gaze to him, not sure how to gauge the look on his face. Was he being serious? Her eyes moved over to his throbbing member; she could tell he was being serious. He was ready to go again, and she was impressed.

Amber couldn't help the smile that spread across her face. She guessed she could stay a little longer.

4

Jack

His nose had been twitching most of the night. Jack was a light sleeper, the tangle of bedclothes behind him a testament to his tossing and turning. He'd gone to the window several times, the sliver of the moon leaving most of the shadows in place. Now, in the pre-dawn hours, the first hints of color spilling across the sky, dispelling the shadows, the night succumbing to the fingers of daylight. This was his favorite part of the day. It's when the day still held promise, and nothing had gone wrong yet. It was still molten, and nothing had set in stone.

Bare-chested, with pajama pants on, he caught his reflection in the mirror. He didn't look half-bad, his build still muscular, arms and chest toned, his abs well defined. He could hold his own against most thirty-five-year-olds in town. Not that he was sweating it. He'd given up on trying to make an impression. He was who he was, and he didn't much care who liked it or not. He was past all that crap.

Taking off his pajama bottoms, he whistled at his reflection and broke out into a laugh. It was time to let his panther free and run. His panther mewled, ready for his time of freedom.

He loved to run in the pre-dawn hours, the time when the world was just waking up and the scents were so strong and pure. As he shifted into his panther, Jack licking the back of his front paw, he inhaled and reveled in the cacophony of smells. Stretching, he arched his back, body trembling in anticipation for the hunt that was about to begin.

He could smell the nearby creek running along the base of the mountain and the rotten leaves left by the previous winter wafting to him on the breeze. He caught the scent of a small gathering of deer further down the mountain and smiled. His heartbeat quickened, pupils dilating, his body tensing like a spring. The muscles moved under black fur, golden eyes catching the first of the dawn's light.

He was a sight to behold.

Lithe, his panther was truly poetry in motion, the light-catching each motion. He felt like the world around him was in slow motion, his panther moving with incredible quickness. As he let out a soft mewl, he caught sight of something to his left. He smiled.

When the rabbit hopped into the clearing, it was on.

Jack's cat leaped at it, crouching down low, chin to the grass, front paws on either side of him, haunches wiggling back and forth. The rabbit froze, looking at him, his nose twitching. Jack growled, the sound low, in the back of his throat.

The rabbit took off, Jack in hot pursuit. The cool kiss of the dewy grass beneath his paws was heaven, his body finding its rhythm, muscles rippling with motion. The rabbit darted to the right and angled beneath some underbrush. Jack reacted, his panther like a well-oiled machine, his claws rending the soft earth as he turned to maintain his pace with the rabbit.

He loved the feeling of being one with the wild, his core, his soul feeling so full and vibrant. Racing after the rabbit, he darted between two trees and cut off its progress, the rabbit changing direction. He chased for a few more minutes before it darted down a hole. Jack then raced back to his house feeling satisfied even though he didn't catch his prey. Coming up onto the deck, he changed back to his human form, feeling so relaxed and ready to face the day.

He got dressed before going inside and good thing, too, as his mom was standing there in his kitchen cooking breakfast, the smell of bacon, sausage, and eggs thick in the air.

He smiled. "What are you doing here?"

His mom smirked and chuckled. "Good morning to you too. It's so great to see you, Mom. Thanks so much for making me breakfast."

He raised his hands in surrender. He never could win with her. Even though he was thirty-five she still had a hold on him.

"Thanks for breakfast, Mom."

"You're welcome. Out for a jog?"

"You could say that," Jack said with a chuckle, sitting down at the table as his mom brought a plate full of breakfast goodness. He dug right in, the rabbit chase made him hungry. As he ate the eggs and bacon, the flavors exploding in his mouth, he suddenly realized something was going on. She didn't visit this early often. He eyed his mom suspiciously.

"So, what brings you here, Mom?"

"Can't a mother come over to her son's house and make him breakfast."

"Sure, she can. But you don't do this kind of thing so early in the morning. Is everything all right?"

His mom waved him off, scoffing. "Oh, please. Everything is just fine." She poured herself a glass of orange juice she had sitting on the counter.

"Then why are you here so early in the morning, making me breakfast. You've never done this for me."

His mom took a deep breath and came to sit down next to him.

He sighed. She was up to something. "What do you want, mom?"

His mother took a drink of orange juice before clearing her throat. "Okay, so there is something."

Of course, there was.

"April wanted to talk to you."

As alpha of the pack and man of the house, it was practice for a young woman from the pack or a female family member to ask permission for certain things.

"What does she want?"

"She wants to head to California with three of her best friends. Two of the girls are werewolves, the other is human. She wants to explore the world a little bit before buckling down on her studies."

Sounded like she didn't want to go to school to him. April was so much smarter than he was and he was really surprised to hear that she didn't want to go directly to the college after school.

"When is she planning on starting college?"

His mom's hesitation made him wonder if April didn't have any plans to go to college after all. Was this all a ruse so she'd not ever have to go to school.

"She said she'd pick up extra shifts at the bar."

"It's not about working at the bar. She's too young to be traveling by herself. Especially to California. That's a lifetime away before she's ready. She doesn't have any support there."

His mom didn't say anything, her judgment clear in her silence. He knew April was growing up. He was so proud of his sister but he also knew the world out there, the world behind his control, beyond his purview. He knew she wouldn't like it, but unless she agreed to take a male escort as protection, he wasn't going to let her go.

"Will you just talk to her? She's your sister."

"Fine. I'll talk to her," he sat his fork down, having lost his appetite.

"Great. She's just outside."

Of course, she was.

His sister came inside, smiling. "Jack."

"Mom told me about your spring break idea."

"It's not spring break," she said sharply.

Jack laughed. "Kinda sounds like it."

"But it's kinda not."

"Look, you're too young to be traveling on your own so far away, okay? There are too many unknowns out there."

He had to give her credit; she didn't roll her eyes at him.

"Do you remember, Samantha?" she asked him.

"Your friend? The one with the horrible tattoo on the back of her hand."

She tucked a strand of hair behind her ear as if she was embarrassed for her friend. It was a horrible tattoo and done on a dare. "Yeah, that's her."

"What about her?" Jack was done listening to his little sister. He had to get on with his day. She wasn't going to California without an escort and that was final, but he was going to listen to her plead her case.

"Well, her big brother is letting us stay at his house. He's lived out there like five years or something and has plenty of room for us."

Jack took a deep breath and considered what she'd said. He puffed out his cheeks as he exhaled. "I'll think about it."

April's face looked like someone closed the curtain, her smile disappearing as her eyes darkened. She didn't say anything, pouting a moment before heading for the door, leaving him in the kitchen.

His mom stepped back into the kitchen, her motions suggesting she wasn't at all happy with what had just transpired. His entire family was so passive-aggressive when it came to confrontation. Was he like that? He didn't think so.

"What?" he asked with raised eyebrows.

His mom turned her gaze to him. "Nothing."

"I know that's not true so why don't we save a lot of time and you just tell me what you're thinking."

"I just think you're being unjustly hard on her because she's a girl."

He scoffed as he walked over to his coffee pot and poured himself a cup, the scent of it enticing.

"You took off to join the army right after high school," she said sharply. "You didn't go to college. You went to see the world. Why can't she do the same?"

He took a sip and shook his head. "It's not the same thing."

"Sure, it is."

"Mom, I went off to serve my country, not run around on a perpetual spring break."

His mom was quiet again.

Jack cleared his throat said in a lowered voice, "I'm just afraid that once she's on her own, she'll get into trouble without someone in authority watching over her."

Her mom finished washing the dishes and tossed the towel over the faucet. "Maybe. But she does need to grow up and she can't learn being stuck at home as if she was on house arrest."

Folding her arms over her chest, she leaned against the kitchen counter, head cocked to one size. Oh, no. Not the dreaded 'Mom' post. That was never a good thing.

"What is it now?" he asked in a softer tone.

She smiled and he was curious what she was up to now. "What's bothering you, son? You've been acting odd since last week. You've been staying to yourself. You've been quiet."

"What are you talking about?" He took another sip of his coffee, not realizing how hot it was, and burned his tongue.

"What's going on? Something's bothering you." His Mom pushed away from the counter and placed her hands on the island in the middle of the kitchen, eyeing him.

"It's nothing, Mom," he replied staring at his cup.

"It's always something. Talk to me. Let me in. Maybe I can help. No matter how old you get, you're still my son and I still worry about you and love you."

A moment of silence elapsed before he said, "I've just been thinking a lot lately. I thought I was happy with the way things are. You know, my life. Where I'm at. All of those things. I hadn't even thought about taking a mate. I mean sure someday I'll take one to continue the family's legacy, but I hadn't been considering it at all until I talked with Tate. He found someone."

His mom moved with calculated slowness, hand tracing the line of the counter. "There are a few single girls in the pack. They'd make good mates."

"I know there are, mother but I'm not interested in any of them. They're too desperate. All any of them do is throw themselves at me. I want someone who's going to challenge me, you know?"

"Well, then why not set up a profile online or something? That's how I find company at night."

His eyes went wide at her admission. "Wow, not the conversation I was expecting to have with my mom today."

"Oh, come on, it's fine. Nothing wrong with a little fun," she said playfully.

Jack cleared his throat, "I think it's great as long as you watch yourself and don't get into any trouble."

"Easier said than done," his mom said, winking at him as she left the kitchen.

5

Amber

Amber needed a break. This job was killing her. It wasn't that she couldn't do the job—hell, a trained monkey could do it—it was more that the grind was getting to her. Even after the great sex she'd had with Rick—three amazing rounds—her stress and anxiety hadn't dropped much at all. In all honesty, it felt higher than before which wasn't a good thing. She had to do something to calm down and just chill out.

She suddenly had a great idea.

Taking out her phone, she dialed Misty.

"Hello?" Misty's voice sounded nervous and apprehensive. A little hiccup of fear surprised her as she wondered if Lyle had found her again.

"How are things going? You getting settled in?" Amber asked, twirling a strand of hair around the tip of her finger.

It was quiet for a moment and Amber knew Misty was nibbling on the knuckle of her right index finger. She did it all the time when she was nervous.

"Yeah. This place was a little bit of a wreck though when I got here. I've been cleaning. Tell your dad he owes me." They both chuckled.

A woman stepped into Amber's office for a moment and said, "Amber, don't forget the meeting in the conference room."

"Shit." She had already forgotten the meeting. Sometimes she hated how efficient Margaret was. She'd been her father's secretary since the beginning of time at least as far as she was concerned. The woman had probably learned how to type on a stone tablet for crying out loud.

"Misty, I gotta go save the world. I'll call you later."

"Okay, talk to you later."

They both disconnected and Amber headed to the conference room cursing herself for not remembering her Coke from the fridge. It would've at least made the meeting bearable. Sad to say, her choice of beverage was usually the most interesting thing in these meetings. They were so long and so boring. She honestly felt a little piece of her dying with each meeting. Amber wanted to just scream but of course, couldn't. After all, she didn't want any blowback from her dad if she did something stupid in this conference meeting.

The meetings were always something that could've been handled in an email. There was no need for everyone to come to except to stroke everyone's ego. It was a waste of time. So instead of just clicking on an email and skimming it for a few minutes, she was bored for an hour listening about last quarter's stats and two new clients the firm had signed.

Standing up from the conference table, gathering her things, and covering up her doodles, her dad asked, "Amber, you got a minute?"

Oh, no. Had he seen the doodles? She hadn't fallen asleep like the last meeting. He should see that as a big improvement.

"How did things go the other night?" he asked.

"What?" her eyebrows furrowed in confusion.

"Your date. You left the restaurant, remember?"

She felt a little rush of excitement go through her remembering that night. She curled her toes inside her shoes. She smiled, "Yeah, I did."

"Well, I was wondering how it went. I have the number of a new shifter who just moved here from the west coast. He's handsome. I promise he's not some hideous freak. Works with some telecommunications company and seems well off."

Her smile faltered. She wanted so badly to roll her eyes but didn't. He hadn't heard anything she'd said the other night. Raising her hand, her dad stopped talking.

"I already have a date tonight."

"Oh?"

"Yeah, so I'm busy." She didn't like lying. She wasn't very good at it. Amber especially didn't like lying to her father. It made her feel like she was ten lying to him about eating cookies before dinner. It was ridiculous. She was twenty-five not nine. Yet, somehow, he still made her feel like a little girl when talking to her.

"The same guy?" Her dad raised his eyebrow which she didn't know if she should take that as a good sign or a bad one. Amber wasn't sure if he was disappointed or hopeful that it was the same guy. The thought of his daughter going out with multiple men at the same time was probably a little too much for his conservative mind to handle. She decided to let her dad off the hook and lie again.

"Yeah. Same guy."

She bit her lower lip and ran her fingers across the back of one of the chairs. Just as she managed to get her emotions in order, her dad sent an ice pick to her heart. He should be famous for the effect he had on her.

"Think I can meet him sometime?" he asked in a curious tone.

Her eyes narrowed. At first, she wasn't sure if her dad was being serious or not. He liked to tease and play practical jokes so was this one of them? Where had that come from? She wasn't prepared for that. Hell, she wasn't even sure she had his contact info anymore.

"Maybe. But, Dad, it's too soon."

"I'm sorry. I just want you to be happy and find someone you can love and settle down with. A mate. I don't want you to turn into your mother."

His words were like cold water on her face, her heart pinched in her chest. It was rare for her dad to say something negative about her mom. Her mouth hung open a moment before she cleared her throat.

The frustrating thing? He wasn't wrong.

She was turning into her mother more every day. She didn't take her romantic relationships seriously just like her mother hadn't. Her mother still hadn't found someone else to be with after divorcing her dad.

"I get it, Dad. Now's not the time." Picking up her things, she left the conference room and headed to her office. Glancing at the clock, she decided she'd put in enough time for this crappy day and left the office.

*****

At her apartment, Amber showered and got ready for her date. She hadn't lied entirely to her dad, but it was a different guy. She hadn't met him, but she craved him, nonetheless. Amber loved men wanting her, aching for her. She got wet just thinking about it.

She went with black lingerie beneath her dress, the color always making her feel even sexier. It didn't take her long to drive to the restaurant where she met her 'date' for the evening. He was cute. Not as muscular as her last hookup but he would do. His skin had the sun-kissed look of someone who worked outside, his blond air bleached.

"What do you do for a living?" Amber crossed her legs getting pressure on her clit as she finished her drink.

"I coach college football. Love watching the players gel as a team and come together. It's so rewarding."

Come together. What a nice turn of phrase. All she could think about was him bending her over the hood of the car and taking her roughly. She had to stop daydreaming.

"Think we could take this conversation back to my place?" She wasn't usually this bold but she wasn't usually this horny either. Who was she kidding? She was always this horny.

He chuckled uncomfortably. "I'd like to get to know you a little better first."

Oh, no. That was the death knell for this relationship. Why was it so hard for guys to understand in this new age of women empowerment there was no need to put on airs and pretend they wanted to fuck as much as the women did. There were no dalliances, no need to put on a good face. Just say what you want and mean what you say.

"Well, I get that, but that's not going to happen tonight." She picked her small studded clutch. "Thanks for the date. I had a really nice time."

"Wait. You're leaving?" he scoffed.

"Yeah, it's okay. The brunette at the bar has been looking over here for the last fifteen minutes. If you play your cards right, I'm sure she'll come over and you can talk to her. I'll call you." She kissed him on the cheek and headed out.

"Oh. Okay. Well, have a good night," he called after her, but she wasn't interested. There was no way she was going to call him back. If he hadn't taken the bait tonight, what was the point?

6

Jack

Sometimes owning your own business sucked. Whenever an extra shift needed to be filled or an inventory needed to be finished it always fell to him. His feet felt heavy coming up the stairs from the basement where the beer was stored. Jack shifted the box in his hands, the bottles clinking gently inside. He paused at the doorway when he heard voices.

"I know. I think we should pack up and head out this weekend."

"Your brother is so cute."

"God, that's so gross. He's my brother. Put it in park and reign it in, already," April said to her friend.

Jack shook his head and headed toward the bar to finish restocking it. As April and her friends talked down at one end of the bar, he unlocked his phone and finished setting up his dating profile. He thought it was ridiculous to be relying on a dating app to help him find a woman, but it would at least get his mom off his back for a little while if he said he had been trying the apps.

Occasionally, Jack glances up to see April leaving her friends at the bar to help customers. She takes their orders and brings out their food when it's ready. Jack had to admit she was a help to have around and was happy to see that she wasn't ignoring her work duties.

He thought about searching for the big brother who was supposedly going to let the girls stay at his house. Was he a creepy perv? What was his intentions when April and her friends came to visit? Should he trust April to take care of herself?

Jack poured a couple of beers and gave them to his customers at the bar before checking his profile to see if he had gotten any responses. It was ridiculous. He was like some high school love-sick teenage boy.

He heard a giggle behind him and realized April was watching over his shoulder.

"Wow, you need serious help with your profile. Nobody's clicking on that."

"Really?" he asked.

"Yeah, really."

He knew he might regret what he was going to say next but he went with it anyway. "Well, if you help me get this profile in order, I might consider letting you go to California."

"Shut up. For real?" her eyes went wide with surprise.

"Yeah, for real. But I'm going to need the address and the brother's name to do some checking."

"Jack. That's. Thank you!"

"I haven't agreed to anything yet."

He knew it was a losing battle. He was going to let her go, he just needed to wrap his head around it a little bit longer.

"Give me your phone and let me fix this sad little profile up a bit." After five minutes, she hands his phone back. "All set. Good luck, brother."

"You fixed my profile that fast?"

"I did. You needed to post a better picture and add more than a few words on your bio, but I think it looks way better than it did."

"Thank you, April."

"Now, am I going to California?"

Jack eyed the door as a small group of people make their way to a table. "How about we talk about it later."

Twenty minutes later, his phone rings. Jack's heart leaps in his chest as he wasn't prepared to start talking to the opposite sex about dating when he sighed a breath of relief. It was Tate.

"Jack, I know you've got a lot on your plate at work but I had to let you know you have something else to add to it."

"Please tell me I've won some cosmic lottery."

"Not the kind you would want to win."

Jack chuckled, "Well, let me in big dawg. What's going on?"

"You remember Lyle, right?"

How could he forget? Lyle was one of the few werepanther outsiders in his territory that was always causing trouble. If he wasn't starting fights with other members of the pack, he was trying to screw their women. He'd been busted a few times for stealing too. It was like the guy lacked any impulse control whatsoever.

"Sure. What did he do now?"

"Well, he is Misty's ex. She'd come up here to Deerskin Peaks to get away from him and he tracked her down somehow. Anyway, since you're the alpha of your pack I wanted to let you know. It's not good."

"What happened?"

"Let's just say things didn't go the way he thought they would and he's in the hospital right now."

Jack coughed and took a drink. "You have something to do with him being there?"

Tate scoffed sarcastically. "What? Me? Not a chance."

"Right," Jack said with a soft laugh.

"Hey, you know how Misty and I have been spending a lot of time with each other, right?"

He knew where this was going. According to Tate, Misty told him that Lyle was a jealous asshole all the way around. If he thought someone was trying to cut in on his action, he'd come down with both feet on whoever it was. Problem was, Tate could hold his own and then some.

"I think something needs to be done. He'll have criminal charges to deal with but I'm talking about pack law."

"I agree with you, Tate. Know what pack he's from?"

"I've already talked to his alpha. His name is Alan. He's from a New York pack. He told me Lyle is going to be banished for life for attacking a human but if he needs to do time for human law that it's okay with him. He left it up to me on how to deal with it. Alan also talked about him having to wear a collar if he didn't abide by their decision."

"Right. I can contact a local coven and see they can spare a witch for an evening to have it placed. Think it's ridiculous that technology hasn't advanced enough yet to still need witches to place the collars."

"Good idea," Tate said.

Deerskin Peaks: Taming the Wildcat

7

Amber

She liked road trips. Most times. This one kind of sucked though. It was still relaxing and a nice change of pace from being stuck in the office, breeze in her hair tunes thumping but she was still worried about Misty. Lyle wasn't good for her and never had been. Misty always talked about how good he was in the sack but no thanks. Amber liked being spanked as much as the next girl, but that was during sex not while sitting on the couch watching TV.

Her phone rang on the passenger seat. Turning down the radio, she picked up and winced. It was her dad.

Sigh.

"Hello?"

"Amber, it's your dad."

Her dad still didn't get cell phone technology. Even though she'd shown him his picture on her phone and how it worked, he didn't get it.

"I know, Dad."

"Oh, okay. Well, I have some bad news."

Lately, whenever he said that to her, Amber's mind immediately went to the darkest places. Her little brother dead. Her mother dead. It was all death. Amber had a horrible realization. She was fast becoming her mother. As much as she wanted to deny it, she was.

"Everybody okay?"

"Oh, sure. Everybody's fine. I just wanted to tell you that the law conference has been postponed."

"Oh." There was no way he was going to ask her to come back to the office. No way. She was going to see Misty. Period.

"I just figured since you were out that way you could check in with the sheriff of Deerskin Peaks. We need to find out what's going on with Lyle. I need you to kind of keep tabs on him and the situation."

Great. So, now, I'm a babysitter? What do I get $10 bucks a night?

"Are you serious? I'm supposed to be up here on a mini vacation visiting my friend to make sure she's okay."

"I know. I just need you to be my eyes and ears there. He's being punished and I just need to make sure he obeys my orders."

"Okay."

"Thanks, hon."

"Sure thing." What else was she supposed to say? "Talk to you later, Dad."

"Okay. Let me know when you get there. Bye now."

Great. Great. Great. Great.

Why did she get stuck doing grunt work? She was above all that nonsense. Who was she kidding? As long as she was living in the same town as her pack and her dad was the third in command, she was always going to be stuck doing stuff she didn't want to.

*****

She drove for another hour before the road began looking familiar. Passing the sign for Deerskin Peaks, she tapped the steering wheel. It had been years since the family had used the cabin but the town hadn't changed all that much. It was still quaint and quiet. There were only a few people out on the streets.

Amber followed the road up the mountain, leaving the small town behind. The woods encroached on the road, the view growing more spectacular with every passing second.

Pulling up out front, she saw Misty and her heart almost broke. Amber was glad she came. Her friend needed her badly.

*****

They talked for almost an hour and after she helped clean the cabin a little more, they went to town, darkness dripping around them. There were a few other people out wandering around but not many. It was a sleepy little mountain town. She was probably going to have a hard time finding someone to sleep with here.

Great.

After walking a few blocks, Misty pointed to the sign for Jack's.

"Jack's?" Amber cocked an eyebrow.

"Don't let the sign fool you. It's good stuff. Tate took me there the other night."

"Did he now?" Amber couldn't help but smirk at her best friend.

"Stop it."

As they walked into the restaurant, a man behind the bar waved to Misty.

"Jack, how are you doing?" Misty asked as they approached him.

"Doing good."

"This is my friend, Amber. Amber this is the aforementioned, Jack."

"Good to meet you." Amber ignored Jack's extended hand and went in for the hug. He was thickly muscled with just the right amount of gray in his hair. There was something decidedly yummy about the way he looked that had her pulse scampering and her sex throbbing.

"You two want some lunch?" Jack asked, his eyes appraising her as she was him. He was trying not to smile but failing.

"Sure, I'll have the club with fries and a Coke." Misty lightly kicked Amber in the ankle to get her attention.

"What?"

"Uh, he wants to know if you want anything."

"Oh, really?" Amber asked, almost purring with seduction, hoping he'd ravage her later. The corner of Jack's mouth went up in a half smile as if he knew what she was thinking.

"To eat, Amber. To eat. Sustenance. Food." Misty whispered loudly.

"Oh, oh. Okay," Amber frowned playfully. "I'll have what she's having."

"Be right back ladies," Jack winked at Amber before he walked toward the kitchen, the swinging door closing behind him.

"Can you be any more obvious?" Misty asked, chuckling.

"He's a yummy mountain man. I have to at least get something out of this lame trip."

"I thought hanging out with me was enough of a reason to come."

"Well, sweetie, you don't compare to being ravaged by a real man."

The two walked to a booth with a view of the street. Amber sat opposite of Misty, but in view of the kitchen.

"Besides, he's one."

"One what?" Misty's eyes narrowed with confusion.

Amber couldn't help but shake her head slightly. Misty could be so obtuse sometimes. Amber took in the room around them to make sure no one was listening in on their conversation before she leaned across the table and whispered, "A werepanther."

"Are you serious?" Misty turned to direct her gaze toward the kitchen.

Amber nodded. "Yeah. And a hot one at that."

Minutes later a young female waitress brought their drinks. "Jack said he will be right out with the rest of your order."

Amber couldn't help but beam with giddiness, to which Misty had to comment on. "You are worse than a high school girl with a crush."

"Oh, hush. Here he comes." Amber's mouth curved upwards into a flirty smile as she watched Jack head their way.

Jack set their plates down on the table, his gaze moved over to Amber, and he grinned as if he had been caught sneaking a cookie out of the cookie jar. He cleared his throat before he said, "Anything else you need, don't hesitate to ask."

"Thank you," Amber purred.

Jack winked at Amber who carefully unwrapped her straw, placed it in her drink and slowly drew the Coke into her mouth, eyes never leaving Jack's gaze. Did he just shiver before walking back to the bar? That made Amber wet, panties clinging in all the right places.

Misty laughed under her breath. "I think the temperature has gone up in here."

"You think so?" Amber asked, turning her attention to her best friend.

"Know so. Goodness. If he doesn't know that you want him already, I may have to have a word with him."

"So, tell me more about your hunky beau. Think it's serious?"

"It is," Misty answered with a sigh.

They finished their dinner as Misty continued to talk about how she enjoyed living here. Amber tried to be invested into the conversation, but she was wondering how to get some alone time with Jack without being a bitch to Misty. Her prayer was answered when Misty said, "I'm going to run a quick errand. I figured you might want to stick around here and do your werepanther mating ritual with Jack."

Amber giggled, finishing her Coke. "You know me too well."

"I'll be back in a few so you won't have time to do anything other than a quickie."

"Werepanthers are like rabbits when it comes to mating. Quick and dirty."

Misty rolled her eyes dramatically and let out a small laugh. Getting up from the table, Jack walked over and asked, "How was everything?"

"Good as always, Jack. I have to run an errand or two. You mind keeping Amber company?"

He looked at Amber and gave her a mischievous grin that said he would be more than obliged.

"After all, she is a city girl out here in the great Wyoming wilds."

"I'd be glad to." Jack started to clear the table as Misty left. "Let me take these to the kitchen and I'll be right back."

After clearing the table, he came back, sitting down across from her. His eyes were a beautiful brown, the goatee framing his mouth perfectly, making his dimples stand out even more.

"So, what brings a city girl like you to Wyoming? It can't be the beer."

Amber chuckled. "Misty and I are best friends. She had to get away from a sticky situation back home."

Jack drummed his fingers on the table before saying, "I heard a little something about that."

"This mysterious Mr. Tate?"

"Yeah. He and I go way back. He's a good guy. He'll take good care of her."

She smiled, some of the stress lifting from her shoulders hearing him say that. She was worried that Misty hadn't taken enough time to breath and soak in her newly found freedom before getting into another relationship.

"I know your father, you know."

"Oh, you also know how to kill the buzz I had going."

"No, it's nothing like that. Look, I just meant that I haven't seen him in a long time. I also remember you when you were younger."

"Oh, so you're a creeper too?"

Jack scoffed, waving his hand at her to dismiss her comment. "God, no. Nothing like that."

She cocked her head to the side and said teasingly, "Right. You were just stalking me all that time until you could take me when I was an adult."

He let out a small laugh. "You are one twisted cat. No, nothing like that. And who's to say I'm even interested in you?"

Amber sat up straight and gave him a shocked expression. This was different. Of course, he was lying. Right? "Really?"

He crossed his arms over his chest and leaned back in the booth. Jack flinched when she put her foot against his crotch feeling how hard he was. His eyes darted up catching hers.

"I think we have evidence that someone is interested in me after all. Are you out? Do they know?"

He shook his head, his smile fading as she continued to massage his cock with her foot. He was throbbing. He was so hot-looking, and she wanted him right now.

"I'm the alpha of a small pack out here. Only ten of us. I keep it quiet. Careful to change."

"For an idiot that's pretty smart."

"What makes you think I'm an idiot?" he scoffed.

"Because you haven't kissed me yet."

"You're fast, you know that?" he said huskily.

"I'd say that you're getting to know me really well," she said.

8

Jack

He had wanted to take her the moment he saw her. The dark hair. Dark eyes. Beautiful body. Jack hadn't been able to take his eyes off of her. She stirred his panther in a way no one had done in years. She was sending out signals that she wanted him too. Hopefully, she was serious and not just toying with him.

Jack didn't want to pressure her into anything and ruin any chance to be with her. He could tell that she was something special and didn't want to ruin it by rushing into something if she wasn't ready.

After she began massaging him with her foot, he asked her to take a walk with him through the woods, the fog hugging the ground in the moonlight. An owl was talking in the distance, insects chirping. He loved the chilled air at night.

"I'm so glad you came."

"Oh, I haven't come yet."

"What?" He was still getting used to her brand of humor but loved when she caught him off guard like that. It made him throb, wondering what she would feel like when he was inside her. Every minute he spent with her so far had him harder than steel. He couldn't wait to knot her. His panther purred.

"I haven't come yet," she repeated. "I hope too soon though."

God, she was killing him.

"I want to show you something. Are you comfortable changing into your panther form and following me?" he asked. He started to pull his shirt off but wanted to wait for her to answer him first. Some shifters were a bit shy, but she surprised him.

She didn't bat an eye smiling as she began to undress before shifting. She was beautiful, her coat a golden brown, eyes to match. He shifted too and together they raced through the forest, black and gold forms in concert with one another. The woods came alive around them, the smells thick and wonderful, the sounds like their own private symphony.

Amber followed him, proving that she was able to keep up with him every step he took. It was dizzying seeing her lithe form moving so elegantly, leaping over fallen trees, racing with him with ease. She was magnificent.

Jack's body was alive with the scents of the forest around him and Amber's sweet scent was intoxicating. It was hard to focus on the path ahead, his eyes watching the muscles moving beneath her golden coat. Leading her deeper into the woods, they crested a hill and he slowed as they moved down the other side.

"What did you want to show me?"

Jack wanted to show her everything. He had never been more certain of who she could be to him, to the pack. But he held his tongue.

"Do you hear it yet?"

She paused, a curious look spreading across her panther face before saying, "Is that water?'

He nodded.

They moved to the cliff's edge so she could get a good view of the waterfall. It roared before them, water tumbling over fifty feet into the mountain stream below.

"It's beautiful."

Yes, she was. He smiled staring at her.

"What?"

"Nothing. Just admiring the beauty of the woods around me."

Amber tilted her head and purred. "Is that what you were admiring."

"Yes, is that a problem."

"Not for me."

He felt his cock rising but didn't want her to notice. "Ready for a swim?"

She blinked in surprise. "Are you serious?"

Jack only nodded and leaped from the cliff, his black panther body shiny in the sunlight as he plummeted into the water below, the wonderful chill was immediate and what he needed to calm his growing erection.

He looked to her standing on the cliff face five stories above him and called, "Are you going to join me?"

"You're crazy."

She wasn't wrong. Being with her made him want to do all kinds of crazy things. He could feel her carving out a place in his heart and he smiled.

"Maybe. Is that a no?" he asked.

Her answer was action. She jumped off the cliff, golden body arching, the moonlight making her coat sparkle. Ripping through the air, she dove into the water ten yards from where he was.

As she swam to the surface, he noticed that she was changing back into her human form. Her hair dark against her skin, water dripping from her nose and chin. He smiled as he changed into his human form too.

"What's next, wild man? Are we going to go hunt for bear?"

He chuckled, her laughter joining his, the waterfall's roar lost as he was consumed by her.

"Isn't this beautiful?" She asked, his eyes never leaving hers.

"You certainly are."

A smile teased her lips as she came closer to him. "You know comments like that will get you kisses."

"Then I better not stop."

"No, you'd better not."

They kissed, the chill of the lake contrasting with the heat he felt with her so close. Their mouths opened, tongues teasing, her body against his. His arousal couldn't be hidden this time.

"What do we have here?" Amber broke the kiss and reached for his member.

"I don't know, what do we have here?"

His hand brushed her bare breast and she inhaled sharply, biting her tongue. She was just as aroused as he was.

Clearing his throat, he said, "We should probably go."

"Think so, huh?"

She stroked him a few times, kissing him once more before swimming toward the shore.

"Yeah, I do." He didn't want to. He wanted to have his way with her but fought the urge to do so. Not yet.

*****

Back at the truck, he felt almost dizzy. His desire was consuming him. Jack struggled with maintaining control, not wanting to overwhelm her with his passion. Obviously, she knew he was aroused by her, she'd felt it with her hand. That thought brought a smile to his face.

As he walked around to the driver's side of the truck, he reached inside to get his clothes, but she stopped him. Amber pushed him against the side of the truck and stood on her tiptoes to kiss him, pressing her body firmly against his. There's no denying what she wanted, one leg wrapped behind his, pressing against him.

Kissing her passionately, their tongues entwined, he picked her up and moved her to the back of the pickup truck. Her brushed a kiss against her lips and said, "Give me a second. I'm not done with you."

She stood there and watched as he lowered the tailgate and climbed up into the back of his truck. He turned around and offered her a hand, which she took, smiling. He helped her up and then walked to the front and pulled a rolled-up blanket out of the toolbox and spread it out. She stepped forward unable to wait a moment longer. Their bodies wet, her damp hair falling against his face, they kissed again, his hand finding her breast.

As they kissed, she moved his hand down between her legs and started moving it in a gentle rhythm, his fingers finding her wetness. They slipped inside easily, and he moaned wanting to be inside her, aching to take her, craving her body.

"Take me, please. Mount me and make me yours. I need to feel you inside me." She was being playful, but the effect was immediate.

He couldn't wait any longer. His member was already fully erect and glistening with his desire.

"Take me any way you want to but please get inside me," she cooed, aching for him.

Helping her lie down, he readied himself between her legs and slid inside easily, her wetness taking him, his fully engorged member throbbing, Amber moving with him in rhythm.

"Yes. God, you're so big," she moaned.

He groaned as he slipped in and out, trying to hold back his excitement. He could be quite rough sometimes and he didn't want to scare her. As his thrusts increased in intensity, she bucked against him harder.

"Please, yes. Harder. God, harder."

"Yes," he said in a rush. He stood up on his knees and wrapped her legs around his waist and gripped her hips, forcing himself inside her even deeper.

"Love that," she purred. "Deeper. Harder."

He pulled out. "Harder, huh? I need you to turn over and get on your knees."

"Oh, yes," she cooed and quickly got on her knees, showing him her ass.

He loved that he didn't have to be tender with her. She moaned loudly when he slammed himself inside her, his fingers bruising her hips as his thrusts grew more frenzied each time he entered her wetness. He slowed his thrusting, feeling his canines lengthening, he leaned down and nibbled across her back, her moans enticing him to bite harder. She shuddered in excitement pushing her hips against him even harder and he moaned.

Hand reaching back, he spanked her as he continued to slide in and out, her wetness drawing him in, urging him to explode.

"Please give it to me. I'm about to come and I want you to come with me. Please, Jack. Please give it to me."

Her pleading voice. Her pliable body. Her wetness gave him no choice. He was past the point of no return.

"Yes, Amber, yes. I'm ready."

They began to tremble against one another as the excitement of the moment consumed them, both. She screamed as he shoved himself deeper inside her than ever before, the sensation making them quake with pleasure until finally, they both fell into each other's arms. They held each other on the blanket, the beautiful afterglow keeping them warm as the night slowly grew older, the stars shining brightly overhead. They both breathed deeply, inhaling each other's scent and those of the woods around them. He didn't want to move. Jack didn't want the spell of the night to be over.

9

Amber

She couldn't help but think about Jack taking her in the back of his truck. It had been incredible. He had satisfied her like no other lover she'd ever had. Everything was just so natural with him. There was no awkwardness afterward and there definitely wasn't anything awkward during. Just his touch had aroused her like nothing before and when he finally entered her, she almost orgasmed. How was that possible?

There was no awkward chitchat after they'd had sex in the truck bed. They'd just smiled at each other and gotten dressed, driving back to town. The whole evening had been incredible.

The waterfall. The sex. Even the cuddling afterward which she typically despised was so nice.

Back at his place, he made them sandwiches and they talked for hours. She felt like she'd known him forever. The connection between them was undeniable. And for the first time, she hadn't felt like running to the hills after being with someone. Amber had wanted to stay.

"I think I should probably get going."

"Do you have to?"

She wanted to say no that she didn't need to but she knew she had to check on Misty. Her friend was a mess. Amber felt a little guilty now taking a love detour when her friend needed her so badly. She was supposed to wait for her to return to the bar. Did Misty eventually go back to the cabin?

"I do. I had a great time. I mean, a really great time."

Boy did that sound lame.

"Me too." He didn't sound convinced. Was he just disappointed she was leaving or was she misreading his interest? Sometimes she hated her head for thinking like that.

"Can we get together tomorrow?" she asked. It was the first time that she wanted to see a guy again.

He smiled, "That'd be great."

The smile made her feel a little better. "Okay. I'll give you a call, okay?

Nodding he kissed her and said, "Sounds good. I'll take you home."

Driving back to the cabin, she felt such euphoria. Amber was genuinely happy at that moment. Pure and simple, the sensation nearly took her breath away. She knew she'd have to pull it together for Misty. She didn't want to make her friend feel worse by her seeming like some love-sick schoolgirl. That wasn't her.

Walking into the cabin, Misty was in front of the fireplace, blanket around her.

"Hey," Amber said, closing the door.

"Hey." Misty grinned looking at her. "Looks like someone had an adventure."

Amber couldn't help but grin back. "I did."

"Did this adventure include some hot kitty cat love?"

Amber laughed, "You know it's hot panther love, right?"

They both laughed and Amber relaxed, glad her friend seemed better than when she'd first arrived.

"Up for some wine?"

"Do I have a werepanther for a best friend?"

Amber laughed again, louder than before grabbing a bottle of wine and two glasses from the kitchen. She opened the wine and poured them both a glass.

"So, tell me about Jack."

"Are you sure?"

Misty nodded. "Of course. I can see you glowing. So, please, spill it."

Taking another sip of wine, Amber said, "I know I just met him but there's something different about him. You know how I am. I'm a do 'em and dump 'em kind of girl."

"Yes, my best friend is a slut. I know."

"Shut up," she said with a laugh.

Laughing she topped off their glasses with more wine.

"This time is different, Misty."

Misty listened taking another drink of wine. "What's different about him?"

"It's just so easy to be with him. He turns me on like no one else ever has. I'm talking panty-melting sex."

"Isn't that messy?"

"Oh, yes. The best kind of messy." They laughed again. "And to think it all started with Jasper Delacroix."

Misty almost spit out her wine, laughing so hard. "Oh, my God. I never did understand why you let him be your first. His greasy hair products. Oh, I couldn't."

"His hair wasn't the only thing greasy on him."

"Oh, God."

"Mr. Johnson was nice."

"He was also thirty-eight and you were eighteen."

"Nothing wrong with a May December romance," Amber said taking another swallow of wine. She was feeling so good.

"That was a January December romance."

That sent them into hysterics. They drank wine and laughed together until well after 2 am.

10

Jack

Jack couldn't stop smiling. He also couldn't remember the last time he'd had sex good enough to pull a muscle in his back but that's what he'd done. Normally, it wouldn't be a problem, but he was rock-climbing with Tate and he kind of had to be on his 'A' game or he could die. So, yeah, the pulled muscle was a problem.

"So, what's been crackin' in town?" Jack asked to get his mind off his achiness.

Tate scoffed and looked at him like he had three heads. "Crackin'?"

Jack shrugged as they readied their lines for their descent. The peak they climbed offered a great view of Deerskin Peaks nestled in the valley below. He stretched his back.

"You doing okay?"

"Yeah, I'm fine, why?" Jack said with a half shrug. He tried not to grumble as he felt like shrugging wasn't the right thing to do.

"Just aren't moving like you usually do. You aren't getting too old for this, are you?"

Jack laughed. "I'm not sure if I should be flattered that you're watching the way I move or I should be pissed because you just called me old."

Tate chuckled, holding the lines as they dipped over the cliff face. Jack could tell he was preoccupied. They normally talked nonstop when they were hanging out together, but he'd been extraordinarily quiet. He knew his friend was probably worried about Misty. He decided to ask.

"How is Misty doing?"

"It's funny. You know? I would never have thought I'd find a mate just by bumping into her at a store, but that's exactly what happened. She's my mate."

"Have you talked about it? About her being your mate?" Jack slipped his gloves back on as they both walked to the edge.

"Yes. I mean we're taking it slow, but I've told her how I feel about what I want."

Jack nodded. He was impressed. Most times, Tate held things close to the vest. He wasn't an emotional guy. Seeing this side of him was something of a shock. "How does she feel about it?"

"She feels the same way. I haven't told her everything. She doesn't know about my bear side, but the time will come when I will have to tell her."

"Just don't push her too far too fast. It's a lot for a human to grasp, you know?"

"It's hard when you've found the one, you're supposed to be with." Tate adjusted his harness and tested the first line.

Hearing those words stirred something in Jack's chest. He felt the same about Amber. They could be so good together.

"Yeah, I get it. I do. I'd just make sure not to rush it. Have you bonded yet?"

Tate shook his head, tightening his climbing helmet. "No, not yet. It's moving in that direction though."

"What about writing to her?"

"Like what, a text?" Tate frowned.

"No, dumbass. Like a letter. Chicks dig letters."

Tate seemed to think about it for a moment. "Might not be a bad idea."

How was he able to give relationship advice to Tate when he couldn't figure out his own? It wasn't that he didn't care for Amber and that the sex wasn't incredible. It was certainly incredible with her. It was more about the politics involved with him possibly wanting to find a mate while he was the alpha.

They rappelled down the cliff face, kicking away from the mountain time and time again only to be drawn back to its surface, their bodies sliding down the lines neatly, in practiced movements.

At the bottom, they packed up their gear and got into Tate's truck, the weather still holding.

As Tate started the truck, he looked at Jack and pulled the stick shift into drive. "I think I'll write her a letter. I used to hate writing in school but I was always pretty good at writing love notes."

"Oh, I'm sure it'll be a masterpiece."

They both laughed as Tate directed his truck down the bumping mountain road, heading toward town.

"What about you?"

"What?" Jack replied.

"You seeing anybody yet? You seem to have a little hop in your step. You holding out on me?"

"Not holding out just not wanting to talk about it necessarily. It's like if I talk about it somehow that might jinx it or something."

Tate laughed, turning the radio on. "What are we, fourth-grade girls?"

"Not that I know of," Jack chuckled.

"Well, let me know what she's like and maybe we can double date."

He knew he couldn't hold out for long. Not with Misty and Amber being friends. He'd rather be the one to tell Tate what was going on rather than Tate finding out in some other way.

"It's Amber," Jack blurted.

"Misty's friend?"

Jack nodded. "It's good, Tate. I mean real good. I know I just met her and all, but I haven't been this happy in a long, long time."

"I can tell."

"Can you now?"

"You're smiling like some high schooler that just felt his first boob."

Jack laughed, triggering Tate's own roar of laughter as they pulled through town.

"Dropping you off at your place?"

"Yeah. I think I might see if Amber wants to go out tonight."

"You gonna ask her to go steady? Check the box if you like me kinda thing?"

Jack snorted, "Yeah, something like that."

As Tate pulled his truck in front of Jack's place, Jack gathered his things. Tate said, "Good luck tonight, Ace."

"Gee thanks, Dad."

Shutting the door, he went inside and put his things away in the closet. He didn't like clutter. Even growing up, his mom never had to ask him more than once to clean up his room.

He unlocked his phone and called Amber, smiling as he waited for her to answer. She was quick to grab his phone and enter her information into his contacts right before she got out of his truck last night.

"Hello?"

He could tell from her voice she was smiling. "What are you smiling about?"

"Oh, some super cute guy just called me and he makes me all hot and bothered."

He chuckled, "Sounds like a special kinda guy to be able to do that."

"I don't know yet. He hasn't asked me to the prom yet. That's the clincher."

"Oh, then you don't want to go to the prom with me then?"

Her laughter filled his ear and he chuckled. "I'll think about it. I might have a better offer on the way."

"Ouch. Icepick in the heart."

"Oh, don't be so dramatic."

He sniffed and pretended to cry. "I just had such high hopes."

"Did you now?"

He could hear Amber shifting her position. "Maybe."

"Well, do tell. What were you setting your hopes on?"

"You, having dinner with me. It's on me."

"Oh, food play. Interesting."

He felt his face turn red, his member stirring. "Nice."

"Thank you."

"So, what do you think?"

"Sure, when did you have in mind?"

"Tonight. I'll shower and then pick you up in say, an hour?"

"That sounds good to me. Do you have time to meet with the second from my pack? Trina is her name. She's coming into town and wanted to interrogate Lyle and wanted to meet up with you."

He nodded on the phone. "Sure, I can do that."

"Great. Thank you. Now go get cleaned up. I can smell you from here."

"I will. I'll see you in a bit."

"Can't wait. Bye." His heart fluttered, feeling like he was in high school again and about to kiss a girl for the first time.

Amber was certainly different, and he knew she was it. His panther stirred, agreeing with him. He needed her.

11

Amber

Jack's place was nice, his mom and sister giving them the entire run of the house. They wanted to give them privacy. She'd thought he was going to take her to a restaurant but was surprised when he brought her back to his place.

He poured her a glass of wine as he prepared the meal, steam rising from the stove, fresh-cut vegetables. She hadn't realized he cooked. At his bar and grill, he had a professional cook prepare all the meals. Something was arousing about watching a man cook for her.

"I didn't know you cooked."

"Well, you ate that sandwich I made you. I don't just own the bar and grill."

"That's fair. What got you into it?" Amber took a drink from her wine glass.

"I always loved cooking. I think I was a freshman or sophomore when I realized I was rather good at it. I'd always wanted to start a restaurant."

"Well, you've done it. You're living your dream."

"I don't have a fancy restaurant. It's more of a bar that serves good food." He wiped his hands on his apron.

"You have a place where people come to eat food. That's a restaurant in my book."

"Yeah, I get it, but it's not quite the same. It doesn't serve fine foods. It's pasta and burgers with chicken fingers for kids."

"And grownups," Amber raised her hand.

"You're right. And grownups." Jack chuckled checking the chicken in the oven and stirring one of the pots on the stove.

"What is this fine delicacy you're making me this evening, Chef Jack?"

"Oh, my darling it's a chicken dish with au gratin potatoes and a glorious salad to start with."

She laughed, feeling more at home.

*****

The meal was wonderful, but the conversation afterward was even better.

"Where do you see yourself in ten years?" Amber asked, the wine making her a little giddy, but she didn't care.

"What are you my high school guidance counselor?" Jack said jokingly.

"Oh, I hated my guidance counselor. She always had to relate everything she told me back to herself. It was like, 'Oh, you would do great as a piano tuner. I played piano until I was sixteen.' Ridiculous."

They both chuckled and poured a little more wine.

"I don't even know for sure if we had a guidance counselor. I mean, I know I saw the name 'Donald Davenport – Counselor' on the door, but I honestly couldn't tell you what the guy looked like. I don't think I ever saw the guy."

"That'd be a nice way to pick up a paycheck. No one knows you're in there. The door is shut. You don't even have to show up for your job. Just keep cashing those paychecks."

"You do know my friend is the law enforcement around here, right? I'd have to turn you in." His face was stern and she sat up a little straighter.

"What? Oh, shut up."

"Not a chance. I gotta keep up with you somehow."

"Well, I say we go back to the bedroom where we can put it to the test."

"Put what to the test?"

"You keeping up with me in the sack."

"I thought we were doing great last night."

"We did. So, let's do it again," she purred.

They carried their wine glasses with them, hand in hand, walking down the short hallway to his bedroom. As they came inside, he went to close the door and she said, "Don't. Leave it open."

"But they could come home."

"Then let them hear what we're doing in here."

"I don't want to scar my sister for life."

"Understood," she replied and closed the door.

Jack smiled, taking a sip from his wine, putting the glass down on the nightstand. She did the same and sat on the edge of the bed. He moved in front of her and she unbuckled his belt. She wanted the smell of him all over her. She loved using her mouth because it was so empowering to her to hear a man moan when she teased him from oral pleasure. Every inch quivering, every fiber of a lover's being reacting to just a flick of her tongue or the gentle pressure of her lips on his skin.

She loved to tease her lovers for quite a long time, but with Jack, she couldn't wait to have him coming for her. She devoured him, mouth full of his erection, his moans intoxicating her making her wetter by the second. She couldn't wait to feel him inside her again, filling her up, making her cry out in pleasure.

Easing her back against the bed, Jack kissed her full on the mouth, the two of them writhing together as he moved on top of her. His mouth kissed a searing trail down her throat and then across her collar bone. His hands teased between her legs, her breath coming faster, her pleasure undeniable.

Slipping her top off, Jack unfastening her bra, the sensation of him electrifying. Slipping her skirt off, he smiled at her.

"No panties?"

"No waiting that way."

Kissing her knee, he slowly made his way along the inside of her thigh, her legs trembling with anticipation. When he kissed the apex of her thighs next, his tongue flicked out, the sensations spreading through her like never before. The feeling was intense, she started to come even before he pushed a finger inside her.

She felt herself clenching around his finger, his lips against her sensitive bud, his member hard and throbbing against her lower legs.

Looking at him with desire in her eyes, she said, "Kiss me."

He growled, the rumbling low in this throat. "Love to."

His mouth found hers and as they kissed as he slipped inside of her, his hard shaft filling her so fully. His movements were quicker than they had been in the back of the truck. She loved feeling how aggressive he was, his mouth nipping at her throat, teasing her nipples as they both writhed against each other.

"God, yes. Jack, please." She felt him expanding inside of her, stretching her until she thought she'd explode, the feelings so intense.

He softly sucked on her shoulder as he rammed his thick shaft home, again and again, his hips gyrating faster. She opened her legs even wider by pulling them up around his waist, letting him in deeper.

"Harder, please, baby."

He obliged, his hips thrusting hard against her, every inch inside her. She knew he was ready. Amber was rapidly approaching the point of no return too.

"God." He started trembling.

"Give it to me. Please. Give it to me baby."

"Yes!" he groaned loudly.

"Now, please, now! I'm coming!" she screamed.

He bucked inside her, his thickness pulsing as she began to tremble, pleasure wracking her body over and over in one sweet wave after another.

She loved being with Jack more than any other man she had ever been with. Loved how he filled her up. Loved the feel of him inside her. She especially loved how he made her feel and not just sexually. Maybe it was because he was a werepanther too. She wasn't sure.

When she the remnants of her orgasm waned, they remained together for a few minutes, bodies entwined. She felt herself start to nod off and decided she'd better get going or else she'd spend the night and she couldn't. Not this time.

Jack was breathing so deeply in her ear; she knew he was asleep. Carefully, she lifted his arm and climbed out of bed, her body thrumming with pleasure. Running a hand down the length of her body, she dipped it between her legs and shivered from the pleasure of her touch. She looked back at Jack sleeping and wanted him again.

Her gaze ran over his body sprawled out in bed, she didn't want to go but knew she had to get ready to meet Trina in the morning. Her panther wanted to stay and take him again though, but one sniff and Trina would know she was with Jack. She didn't need her father hearing about it before she said anything to him.

Amber watched Jack sleep a few minutes longer while standing in the doorway of his bedroom, her legs rubber. They threatened to buckle as she made her way home. She loved when her legs felt that way after having sex, but Jack made her feel even better.

12

Jack

He stretched beneath the tangled sheet and comforter, his panther purring in that sweet way when it was sated. Turning over, he expected Amber to still be there in bed with him, but she wasn't. He propped himself up on his elbows and looked around the room, wondering if she was in the bathroom. Listening, he could tell she wasn't.

"Amber?" He could tell no one else was home.

He looked on the nightstand on her side of the bed but there was no note, no anything. Jack checked his phone too. No messages either. His heart felt clouded. Was she having second thoughts about them being together? Or was she only looking for a fun night of great sex.

He showered, the hot water washing away his doubts. Walking to the bedroom with just a towel, he heard his phone chirp. Unlocking it, he smiled. It was a text message from Amber.

Went to pick up Trina. I'm dropping her by the bar. After I do that, I have to pick a couple of things up but then I'll come back around to see you.

He quickly replied. Okay. Looking forward to seeing you again.

He wanted to say more than that. He wanted to ask her why she'd left the way she had. Had he done something wrong? Had he not picked up on some signal she'd sent? Jack wasn't good at this kind of thing. He wasn't good with women. They were too complicated. He liked dealing with men. They were straightforward. No games. No tricks. And, certainly no hidden signals.

He didn't want to seem too clingy but what else was he supposed to think. He loved sex with her. It was incredible but he also knew there was something more to her than just that. She was exciting to be around. Even talking to her was arousing. He had never had that with a woman before.

Jack hated what she'd done to him. She had him all mixed up. He was in love with her or at least he'd thought he was. And here he was like some forlorn schoolboy pining away for a girl who didn't care what he was feeling. How could she? She'd just left. No note. No anything.

What was holding her back? What was bothering her? He needed to stop doing this to himself and simply enjoy her company.

*****

An hour later he was at the bar, still grumbling about Amber. He didn't want to have to play nice with Trina, but she was sent from Lyle's pack under the orders of Amber's father and their alpha.

He didn't know what he'd expected to walk into at the bar, but it wasn't the sexy, athletic-looking brunette with green eyes. She walked with a confidence that exuded sexiness with every step. He knew right away she was trouble. She was sexy and beautiful, and she certainly knew it. Trina also wanted everyone else to know it too from the short tight dress she wore that hugged her curves in all the right ways.

"Hi," Amber said, his panther flaring a bit at the sound of her voice.

"Hey."

"This is Trina."

"Trina, it's good to meet you."

"Pleasure's all mine." Her voice was sweet like honey. She shook his hand but held it just a little too long, Amber rolling her eyes. Jack tried to hide his smile. He was glad Amber was a little jealous. Maybe it would wake her up.

"How long are you going to be in town?"

"Might be longer than I thought," Trina said, leaving the strong hint that it was because of Jack.

"I know Tate will be here in a few minutes to talk about what happened. He's the local sheriff. Good people. He was involved in the attack, too. Lyle had been assaulting his ex-girlfriend, Misty when Tate stepped in and saved her. Was messy business."

"I bet it was," Trina said again in her honey-sweetened voice. "Always a shame when one from the pack goes bad."

He knew what she meant. Rosario was a member of his pack that had gone bad about a decade back. Started slaughtering local cattle and sheep, tearing through them by the score over several months. He was finally shot and killed by a local farmer who'd simply had enough.

"So, Jack if I were to need your assistance later could you come by and tuck me in?"

Jack chuckled. "I'm sure you could find plenty of guys to tuck you in."

"Oh, I wasn't meaning you would be the only one to do it. I mean I am a full--service kind of girl; you know what I mean?"

His hardness said he did, but he didn't voice any of those thoughts. He could tell Amber was a little uneasy from her tense body poster and her pinched up facial expressions each time Trina said something naughty.

"While you're in town you'll be okay to shift at the eastern edge of town and up along the mountain passes," he added, changing the subject.

"Thank you. That's good information to have."

"Just want to be helpful." Jack smiled at her and realized Amber was glaring at him. His smile faltered a bit. He uncomfortably shifted back and forth on his feet.

"I'm staying at this western-style hotel. It's horrible. So gaudy and it takes itself way too seriously."

"Oh, you mean the Wagon Wheel Hotel?"

She chuckled, "That's the one."

"It is a little gaudy, isn't it?"

"A little?" She laughed and touched his arm, leaning in a bit to show him her cleavage. "You should come by for a drink tonight."

He waved her off. "Thank you but I'm awfully busy with everything going on."

"Some other time then."

"Thanks."

Amber cleared her throat. "I think we should probably get going."

Jack needed to clear something up first. "Can I talk to you a minute please, before you go, Amber?"

She looked at him and he couldn't read her eyes. Was she angry? She gave him a pensive smile and said, "Okay."

He took her by the arm gently and opened the small storeroom next to his office. He closed the door behind them and pushed her against it. He quickly pressed his lips to hers and kissed her passionately. She didn't fight him, but she didn't lean into him either, her lower body pressed against his driving him crazy. He wanted to take her right then and there, but he didn't. It was so hard to stay in control but somehow, he managed.

"I'm sorry. I just needed it," he said once he broke away from their kiss.

"Look, that's fine, but I'm warning you now. Trina has a way around guys. I didn't like that little sideshow you had going on in there either, okay?"

Chuckling, he touched her arm but she slapped it away. "What? Are we jealous?"

"Maybe," she shrugged.

Taking her palm, he pressed it against his hard member and said, "This is because of you, not Trina. You left me hanging last night, taking off while I was asleep."

Stroking him through his pants, he groaned and then kissed him passionately. "I want you so badly, but I have to take Trina back to the hotel room."

"It's okay I have to get the bar ready for the lunch crowd anyway."

He wanted to bend her over so badly and just ram his cock home not taking no for an answer just to hear her moan, but he didn't. Instead, he gave Amber and Trina a few minutes to leave and jacked off in the storeroom thinking about how good it felt to pin Amber down last night, stretching her out with his thick member.

13

Amber

Trina purred, "That Jack is one hot kitty cat."

She nodded noncommittally. Amber was not at all comfortable talking to Trina. It was like she was always fishing for something or had some hidden agenda for every interaction. She didn't like her at all. She especially wasn't going to talk to her about Jack.

"That stud cannot be single."

She didn't answer, prompting Trina to nudge her arm.

"What?" Amber asked.

"So, spill the beans already. I'd love to have him mount me like the horny slut that I am. Are you kidding? I bet he's a real tiger in bed if you know what I mean. Is he banging anybody? He is married? What? Spill already."

"No, he's not married."

"Oh, my. Then I have to get my claws into that one."

Amber took a deep breath, jealousy rising. She's never been jealous, not like this. No, this was something entirely different, something completely alien to her.

Stopping in front of the hotel, Amber had to hide her smile. The Wagon Wheel hotel was a full-on, very western gaudy motif. It suited Trina well enough with her own ridiculous style.

As Trina got out, she turned to ask Amber something, but Amber floored it, not wanting to hear anything else she had to say especially if it had something to do with Jack again.

Her mind was awash with all sorts of thoughts, some bad, some really, really awful. She ran her finger between her legs thinking of how Jack had kissed her there last night and moaned. She had to get out of her clothes, shift, and run off some of this steam. It was unbearable.

Driving up through the mountains, she wished she'd thought to bring her iPod so she could let some loud music blast her mind clear. Finding a clearing, the sun shining high and bright, she parked and got undressed. As she put her clothes on her seat, she shifted, loving the little thrill it gave her.

Chasing rabbits, she lost herself in the fluid motion of what she was doing. There were no misunderstandings. There was no confusion. There was only her body alive with the scents, sounds, and sights around her, the woods accepting her as one.

Climbing the paths through the woods, chasing whatever woodland creatures she could, she arrived at a peak and stopped, looking down at Deerskin Peaks. Spotting Jack's bar easily, she smiled, her heart skipping a beat. Amber could feel her heart swell with the thought of being with him. It was a sensation she hadn't felt in years. She didn't think she would ever feel it again.

She couldn't wait to see Jack again. Feel his touch. Taste his mouth.

After what felt like a few hours, she dressed quickly and got back into the car, heading back to town. She wanted to see him. She needed to see him.

14

Jack

April was almost trembling in the passenger seat because she was so excited to be going to California. It was cute and a little unnerving at the same time. He knew between her three friends and the older brother of one of them, she would be taken care of, but he still worried. She was going to be so far away from anything familiar, but maybe that was the point. He needed to learn to trust her.

"April, I want you to text me and let me know you're doing okay every day, okay?"

"Come on, you've got to be kidding. Mom didn't even make me do that."

"You're my responsibility as your alpha."

"You're my brother."

"And your alpha."

"This is ridiculous. You're not my dad."

"You're right. I have more authority over you than that. I'm your protector."

"Oh, please." She stuck her nose back in her phone, presumably texting her friends they were going to be seeing in five minutes at the airport.

"April, I need you to hear me."

"I'm listening." Her voice had a touch of annoyance to it.

He pulled over and stopped, the terminal still some distance away. It took April a moment to notice the car wasn't moving.

"What gives?" she asked in a tone that said she was annoyed.

"Look at me," he said in a sharp tone.

With a huff, crossing her arms over her chest, she glared at him. "What? I told you that I was listening."

"I can force you to obey if it comes to that." He frowned and looked at her with hard eyes, so there was no doubt how serious he was.

"Come on, Jack. I just want to have some fun," her voice cracked.

"And you will," he said a little softer. "But you need to do as I ask, or this isn't happening."

"I got it." She looked down at her phone again. Taking his finger, he raised her chin, so she had to look him in the eye. She sighed, "I do. I get it. I'll text you every day."

Jack put the truck in gear and drove, pulling into the terminal parking lot. Finding a spot in the front, they gathered her luggage and headed to the terminal. The wind had picked up a bit and he was a little jealous that his sister was going to be basking in the California sun.

April saw her friends and the three of them ran toward each other hugging and squealing. The parents of the other girls waved to him as he approached. Less than an hour later, Jack stood with those parents at they watched the plane racing down the runway, picking up speed. He felt like a bit of an outcast, the other parents talking to each other and not including him in their conversation. Jack was all right with it. After all, was he going to see any of these people again? Not likely.

He took a deep breath and hoped he'd made the right decision and that April would to as he asked. He wanted her to know that he would be there if she needed him, especially if she had gotten herself into trouble. He had to hope that she would call him if she did.

*****

Back at the bar, one of his employees had left early for the night, handing him her register drawer. Just as he was getting ready to take the drawer back to the office to count it, the door opened, and someone walked through the door he wasn't expecting at all.

"Mitchell?"

"Hey!" His friend called out, both fists punching the air above his head.

He smiled, not exactly sure how to take his friend's appearance. He'd been suffering from PTSD for years and Mitchell seemed to genuinely struggle with making it through each day.

"Grab a seat. I'm going to take his drawer back to the office, but I'll be right back, okay?"

Mitchell grinned, "Sounds good."

"Mindy?" he called one of his employees. She looked in his direction. "Pour this man a beer please."

She walked over and started talking with Mitchell as he walked to the office. He was tired and not looking forward to dealing with Mitchell. It had been a long day and he just wanted to go home, possibly watch some football, and have a couple of beers before calling it night. He didn't want to have to babysit Mitchell to make sure he didn't get into any trouble. Mitchell had a bit of an anger management problem.

He cared for the guy, he did, but there were only so many times he could bail the guy out of trouble. Mitchell was dealing with bad PTSD from the Army and Jack cut him a ton of slack. The guy needed someone who would help him walk the line.

Counting the money, the knock at the door made him lost track.

"Come in."

It was Trina. She pushed herself inside his office.

"Come on, Trina," he said with a soft laugh. "I'm working here."

"This'll only take a sec. You are so cute when you get a little worked up."

"Trina," he said, feeling a little irritated.

Holding up her hands, Trina sat on the corner of his desk, as he counted the money. He verified the total and slipped the money into a deposit bag.

"I have a hotel room. I wish you'd come over to inspect it for me. Make sure I'm safe."

"Glad you found the hotel." He was doing his best to keep her at an arm's distance. He didn't want her to get the wrong idea. Especially not with Amber in the picture. That's all he needed was to have Amber think something was going on with him and Trina.

The hem of her skirt slid up her legs as she crossed them sitting on his desk. He could see the top edge of her stockings. Jack immediately looked away.

"Oh, come on, Jack. You can look all you want. You know it doesn't bother me."

He sighed, "It bothers me."

"Why don't we grab a bite to eat before we have to get down to business tomorrow?"

"I don't think so. I'm not interested."

"Well, your dating profile says otherwise, stud."

Putting the deposit bag in the safe, he closed and locked it, checking the handle.

"You have the combination to unlock my safe anytime you want, Jack."

How was she bold saying all this stuff? Did it work on guys? Jack figured it probably did. Men were kind of a sad species most time. Then again, Amber was saying the exact same thing and it was working.

Clearing his throat and rubbing his chin, he said, "Trina, I have to get back to work, okay?"

Walking around the edge of his desk, she stuck her leg out in front of him, blocking his path. Standing up, she pressed him back against the wall, her body pressed against his. He tried pushing her away, but she used her werepanther strength to push against him even harder. Trina's mouth found his, her strength prolonging the kiss way longer than it should have been.

Jack pushed back against her even harder, breaking the kiss, a smirk on Trina's face. "Nice kiss, sailor."

Turning around seductively, she walked out of his office and right to the bar, sitting next to Mitchell.

Perfect.

Guilt stabbed at his heart, thinking about the kiss and Amber. Was there anything he could've done to avoid the kiss? He should've tried harder to get Trina out of his office. He realized what she was trying to do once she sat on the corner of his desk. He didn't want to be dealing with her now, too.

15

Amber

She couldn't believe it. Not Jack. Stomach in knots, she'd seen Trina and Jack kissing in his office. Amber had wanted to surprise Jack by stopping by but had been shocked seeing the two of them through his open office door kissing.

Why was she so hurt by it?

Amber shouldn't have been surprised. Men were all the same. They just wanted someplace to keep their dicks warm. She'd just thought Jack was different. He'd said all the right things and made her feel all the things she hadn't wanted to feel before. The things she had protected herself from.

She deserved it. The heartache. The icicles sprinkling across her heart. Amber had wanted to believe in love, in what she felt when she was with Jack. But it was a lie. He'd proven that.

So, here she was packing to head back home, Misty pacing by the open door to the bedroom.

"Are you sure you are okay?"

Amber was so close to tears she didn't know what to say. Anything but the truth. She didn't want to let Misty know she'd been tricked.

Suitcase open, she wasn't even bothering to fold the clothes, shoving them in wherever they would fit. She just needed to get out of here and back home.

"Yeah, everything's okay. I just need to get home. Grandma took a fall and needs some looking after. That's all."

She surprised herself with how easily she lied. Misty didn't deserve that, but she couldn't bring herself to tell her about Jack.

"I can drive you to the airport if you want and take care of the rental for you."

"No, that's okay. I just want to clear my head and besides, I'll turn it in at the airport."

Misty nodded, hugging her. "Thank you so much for coming out to see me. It helped."

"I'm glad. Tate sounds like a great guy. You deserve it."

"Thank you." Misty helped her take her things down to the car, shutting the trunk. Hugging her one more time, Misty said, "Safe trip."

"Thanks. I'll call when I get home."

"You better."

Waving, Amber got into the car and headed to the airport, her phone ringing before she was halfway down the mountain. It was Jack. She didn't answer, hearing the voicemail alert go off. Rolling her eyes, she pushed play to listen to it.

"Hey, I was hoping we could grab dinner tonight. I was thinking Italian but am open to suggestions. I can't wait to see you. Give me a call."

She deleted the voicemail and turned off her phone without replying. She'd had enough. Amber was done. Fighting back the tears, she left Deerskin Peaks in her rearview mirror arriving at the airport forty-five minutes later.

After buying her ticket, she texted William, knowing her little brother would pick her up when she arrived. He was always there for her, just like she was for him. When her friends complained about their little brothers while growing up, she never could figure it out. She and William had always gotten along, never letting each other down. Not like Jack.

Taking her seat, she put in her earbuds and listened to music, and although she didn't think it possible, Amber fell asleep until the plane landed. Feeling that odd sort of disorientation when waking up in a strange place, she walked through the jetway to the airport and picked up her luggage.

Yawning, she pulled the case behind her hoping her brother was on time. As she turned the corner, entering the main section of the airport she realized her brother was more than on time.

He was awesome.

Dressed in a Hawaiian shirt and flipflops, he held up a sign that read, "Prostitution Outreach Program: Free Rides"

She burst out laughing and gave him a big hug. It felt good to laugh.

"You look well-traveled."

William took a bow. "It's this great work-study program I found."

"I see. Prostitute Outreach Program, huh?"

"Oh, yeah. The people are so friendly."

"I bet."

"Free reach around in every class. Met three guys already."

"William." She slapped his arm playfully as they headed to the parking lot.

"So, I have some more good news."

She frowned as they made it to the garage. "Really?"

"We have the castle all to ourselves. The Lord and Lady of the manor have left on a cruise to survey other lands to conquer." William said it with a stiff-sounding English accent unlocking the trunk. They both loaded her luggage into the trunk and then got in the car.

"It would appear as if milady could use a massage, wine, and a nap."

They laugh together as he pulled away from the airport.

"Maybe not in that order. Wine and sleep today. Massage tomorrow."

"And so, it shall be."

16

Jack

His panther side was irritated at the moment. He couldn't get Amber out of his head, but he also couldn't get Trina's kiss out of his head either. It was the latter that had his panther all worked up. How had he let that happen? He wanted to be with Amber, not Trina.

Why hadn't Amber called him back yet?

His heart was pinched with concern, his mind wondering if he'd said something wrong. Had he done something the last time they were together that she didn't like? She'd told him she'd needed to get Trina back to the hotel, but she seemed receptive to his advances.

So, what was going on?

Jack knew he needed to burn off some energy. If he didn't get this out of his system, he wouldn't be able to sleep and stay up all night thinking about all this stuff.

The night around him was saturated with darkness and delight. He could smell the animals in the night, some of them small, a few of them larger. He undressed, the cool kiss of the air making him shiver a moment before shifting into his panther, the night coming to life. A slight growl escaped him before he tore off into the night.

Chasing a fox, he let it escape before scenting a deer. He needed to feed. He needed to give in to his animalistic side and let his panther take over. Racing after the deer, his panther thrilled by the chase, he could feel the passion and longing for bloodlust. He moved in for the kill. Darting over a fallen tree, his panther moved in and leaped upon the deer's back. It fought to free itself underneath him, but his claws sank into her haunches, his front paws twisting the deer's head around a moment before his fangs sank into her. The blood burst into his mouth and he enjoyed every moment of it, rending flesh from bone, relishing the taste.

When he finished, his stomach full, his spirit satisfied, Jack curled up in a grassy patch nearby and took a nap. He dreamed about his father and woke up smiling. He hadn't thought about his dad in a long time and truly missed him. What kind of advice would he offer him right now?

Getting dressed, he walked to the top of the mountain and took in the view, the town stretching beneath him, the stars starting to make their appearance overhead.

He took a deep breath and then headed back home, checking his phone. Amber hadn't answered any of his text messages or calls.

He wanted to scream. Why had he let her into his heart? He knew she was trouble from the start. Not for her, but for him. She was beautiful and exotic looking. The most beautiful girl he'd ever been with and a werepanther too. He knew his father would be proud of him.

He decided to stop in and visit Misty. Maybe she had some answers.

The entire way to Misty's cabin, he kept second-guessing himself. Would Misty even be honest with him if he asked about Amber? He knew they were best friends. Would she even let him in?

He didn't have to wonder long, pulling into the little turnout, parking his truck, he didn't see Amber's car. Maybe this wasn't such a good idea.

Misty opened the front door and stepped out, the interior light spilling across the porch and into the surrounding grass. She smiled. Well, at least she was welcoming him in.

He got out of his truck and said, "Hey, Misty."

She smiled. "Wondered how long it would take you to come see me."

Chuckling, he felt kind of sheepish. "You did?"

"Yeah. Want some coffee?"

He shrugged, walking up the steps, hand on the banister. "Couldn't hurt."

"Come on in."

After pouring a cup for both of them, they sat together on opposite ends of the couch. "Well, I'm guessing you're wondering where Amber went, right?"

He nodded sipping his coffee. "She's not answering. I've tried voicemail and text."

Putting her mug on the coffee table, she nodded slowly. "She went back home to New York."

"Why?"

"Look, Jack. I think you need to talk things over with her. I don't want to get in the middle of things with you two. I've done that kind of thing before, and it was a disaster. It seemed as if something happened and she just left without saying what was wrong."

He knew she was right, but since Amber wasn't there at the moment, he didn't know what else to do.

Finishing his coffee, he said, "Thanks for letting me know, Misty. Means a lot to me. I don't know what happened either, but I would like to find out."

"You're welcome. Will you do me a favor though?"

He looked at her as he stood up. "If I can."

"Don't push her too hard. She's not talking with you for a reason. When she's ready she'll talk."

Jack wasn't happy that Amber left before talking. He didn't know what he did to upset her. Why did he have to be the patient one? Patience was not his strong suit.

"I won't hurt her," Jack replied and released a deep sigh. "I have to help get the bar ready to close."

"I understand."

He did his best to keep his emotions in check. He was wracking his brain trying to go over everything. Was Amber upset at him for how he responded to Trina's advances?

On the way to the bar, he noticed Trina walking in the door. She noticed him, too, and smiled, winking, and licking her lips suggestively.

He shook his head in irritation. Doesn't she ever give up?

He didn't have time for this. It was just one more thing he didn't want to have to deal with on top of worrying about Amber and his sister, April.

Walking up to the bar, he could see she had a short miniskirt on with stockings and high heels. She looked like a hooker but who knows, maybe that was the look she was going for.

"So, how are things going?" she purred.

"Trina, I don't have time to—" he said sharply, but she didn't let him finish his sentence.

"I just wanted to come back and tell you I was sorry for what we did in your office. I'm so very, very sorry. I'd love to make it up to you in a very special way."

"I'm not interested."

"I know that's a lie," she said loudly. Her tone changed as if she was done flirting.

He frowned, his anger starting to rise. "What are you talking about?"

"You're still dating."

"What are you talking about. No, I'm not. I'm with Amber."

"Interesting," she said, giving him a coy smile.

He knew she was just baiting him, but he wanted to know what she was going on about. "Okay, I'll bite. What the hell are you playing at, Trina?"

"Oh, don't play coy with me, stud. I know you play around."

"You've lost me again."

"I saw your profile still up on the dating app. Sly devil. You're gorgeous, a were, have a great physique. How much action *are* you getting?"

He looked around to make sure no one heard her, Trina's voice getting a little louder than he wanted.

Growling, the sound low, rattling his chest, he said through clenched teeth, "I'm not even using the stupid thing. I don't sleep around like you think I do."

"Right. Right. That's what every attached man says when they get caught. Look, I was just letting you know you can have me any which way from Sunday. I think we can be wickedly good together. So, do yourself a favor and call me."

He snarled and stormed away from her, heading to his office. Was that what Amber was mad about? Did she think he was still dating other people even after the amazing time they'd shared? How could she think that?

Walking into his office he whirled around and slammed the door, noticing Trina heading his way. He had zero time for bullshit right now. Jack locked the door, not wanting a replay of what had happened the last time Trina was in his office. God, he wanted to punch something but couldn't find anything suitable in his office.

He sat down at his desk, puffing out his cheeks as he exhaled, opening the dating app. He was going to delete it when he noticed Amber's picture on there. She was looking to hook up and nothing else according to her profile. Seeing her photo, emotions unleashed an uneasy sea in his stomach. Was she seeing other people? Was that what was about? How could she do this to him, to them? Had he meant nothing to her?

Instead of punching something, he threw his cell phone across the room relishing the sound it made when it crashed into the far wall dropping to the floor behind some filing cabinets. Shoving everything off his desk in a frenzied motion, he roared, trembling with rage.

He heard a soft knock at the door.

"Who is it?"

"Just me, boss. Heather. I heard a big crash in there and was just checking to see if you're okay." Her voice was timid and uneasy. She was a great employee who always took great care of her customers.

"I'm fine."

"I can get Tate to come over if you want."

"I said, I'm fine!" His voice almost cracked he yelled so hard.

"Okay. Sorry."

Heather's soft voice strummed the guilt in his heart but it did little to satiate the anger he felt at seeing Amber's dating profile active on his phone.

Shit.

His phone.

He got up and walked over to the filing cabinets, grabbing the broom on his way. He'd need something to help fish it out from behind there. Jack wondered how broken the phone was going to be.

Sigh.

God, he hated the bullshit that came with loving someone.

17

Amber

She'd picked a guy from her dating app for some company tonight. The word company wasn't what she was looking for. She only wanted a warm body in her bed and a firm dick inside her for the next two to three hours.

She hoped he'd be hot and wasn't disappointing.

True to form, Devon was ruggedly good looking, but he wasn't only window dressing. He was smart too. Day trading, Devon had made mountains of money. Not that she cared all that much. She had her own money and wasn't looking to settle down with anyone just yet. Keep it light. Keep it simple.

While listening to Devon, she thought of Jack and her inner panther scowled at her, giving her a tender flicker between her legs. She bit her lip and smiled, not realizing Devon had noticed.

He cleared his throat. "Are you okay?"

She cursed herself for not being more careful. Amber hadn't wanted Devon to notice what thinking of Jack had done to her.

Amber did her best chuckle and gave him a sexy look as if it was Devon that made her react the way she did. At least she thought it was a sexy smile. She had no idea how she appeared at this moment but it seemed to bring about the same result. She didn't want small talk and didn't want to waste time. Amber was horny and in need of a good man. Was he the one? She smiled.

"Would you like to get out of here?" she asked in a sultry tone.

"What did you have in mind?" he asked, the corner of his mouth going up in a half smile.

Devon seemed to be trying to pretend to be surprised. That moment right there sealed it for her. She knew Devon had wanted this to be quick and clean too.

"Up for a drink at my place?" Devon asked.

She smiled. The look had worked, yet again. She let her finger trail up the length of her thigh, teasing between her legs just a minute. She giggled.

"I'd like that."

Devon smiled and stood, pulling her chair out for her. He was even a gentleman. What a bonus. Most guys nowadays didn't think of those things. They all talked about empowering women and women's rights and all that but at the heart of it, the whole thing was bullshit. They didn't care about any of that unless it got them laid. Which was probably the case.

She didn't care about women's rights. Okay, so that wasn't true but she didn't give a shit about them at this moment. She wanted to get laid and get laid now. The rights stuff could wait for another day.

He had a nice BMW, high-end. They made small talk for a few blocks until he pulled over in front of a nice apartment building. Walking around to her side, he opened the door for her, and they headed up to his fourth-floor building.

Inside, he kept the lights low and put on some soft music. "Would you like some wine?" He held up two wine glasses and shook them gently.

She smiled. "Maybe in a little bit?"

"Sure."

Sitting together on the couch, he pushed her hair off her shoulder and kissed her behind the ear. She shivered, inhaling sharply as that little flutter between her legs tantalized her further.

He kissed her earlobe, flicking it with his tongue. Continuing to move closer to her mouth, his kisses teased her cheek even as his hand lazily teased her thighs, fingers feather light.

Amber reached for his crotch, massaging him through the pants, feeling the firmness in her hand. It felt massive and she could feel herself gush. She couldn't help it.

Jack's face blossomed in her mind, and she sat up straight leaning away from Devon. He politely caresses her bare arm, the strap slipping down along her arm. Her body was aching for cock, but she knew it wasn't going to happen. Not now. Not with Devon.

"Are you doing okay?"

She didn't answer, just looking down at the floor not sure what to say. All she could think about was Jack and how wonderful he made her feel. She wasn't feeling any of that with Devon.

He touched her shoulder and said, "We can just chill and hang out if you'd rather."

It made her heartache with how sweet Devon was being. She wanted to explain everything to him but decided not to.

"I'm just feeling a little sick, that's all."

"I can give you a ride home."

Smiling, she squeezed his thigh and said, "No, no, that's okay. I can manage."

"You sure?"

"Yeah. Thanks, Devon. This was nice. Just what I needed."

Amber couldn't read the look on his face and didn't need to she supposed. It was a mixture of sadness, disappointment, and crushed hope. It took all her strength to walk out.

"Take care, Amber."

She could hear it in his voice. He knew they weren't going to see each other again which was probably a good thing. If she did, she'd probably do something stupid like fall in love with him, too.

Downstairs, she walked out into the night air, and inhaled, her inner panther purring with the possibility of being set free with all the scents wafting around her. Raising her hand, she hailed a cab and climbed in, giving the driver the address. She was going home.

Thinking about Jack again, she wondered what he was up to. Was he dating too? Had he asked Trina out? Or had they just fucked? She didn't care one way or the other, but she hated that she couldn't get him off her mind. Amber had gone out tonight to get him off her mind, to just let loose and have some fun with someone, and instead, here she was feeling miserable back home.

Fighting with her key for a moment, she walked in and found William and one of his friends playing X-box, the volume way too loud. Her head was pounding.

"Can you turn it down?" she shouted over the noise.

William paused the game, ignoring his friend's protest, and turned toward her. "What are you doing home so early?"

She shrugged.

"Come on, what happened. It couldn't have been that bad, right?"

"My date was fine. It was me that wasn't fine."

"Geez. That bad, huh?"

"I'd rather not talk about it."

"Understood."

She headed for her bedroom when William asked, "Hey, do you wanna go out tomorrow night. Blow off some steam. Mom and Dad are going to be back tomorrow."

"Sure. That might be good."

"Sweet."

She smiled as she shook her head and rolled her eyes.

"What?" he asked with a soft laugh.

"You and your word choice."

"Oh, come on, sweet is cool."

"Please. Sweet is dated just like you are with that lame Hawaiian fashion theme you got going on there." She waved with her hand, motioning up and down his body.

"Hawaiian never goes out of style, babe," he scoffed playfully, his friend nodding his head.

"Keep telling yourself that and you'll never find someone to share your life with."

"Ouch," William's friend said.

Amber went into her bedroom and shut the door, hoping she could sleep without Jack poking his way into her dreams.

18

Amber

Her parents made it back home just after lunch, her stepmom going on and on about all the wonderful places they visited while in the Caribbean. There was no interrupting her and no derailing her. You just had to grin and bear it.

Amber's thoughts tumbled as she feigned interest. She'd learned long ago how to nod in the right places even if she wasn't completely paying attention. The idea of going on vacation suddenly seemed very appealing. Maybe a change of scenery was exactly what she needed. She'd traveled on her own before. William was dutifully nodding at his stepmom and winked at Amber. Amber wondered if he might like to come along with her on a trip. He was always good at picking out a man or two or three to keep her occupied.

God, she needed sex in the worst way.

"Well, how did your trip go? Misty holding up, okay?" Amber's dad asked.

She stopped rubbing her temples and sat up a little straighter, realizing her dad was talking to her. "Yeah, it was good. She seems like she's working through it."

"How's the cabin?"

Amber wasn't about to tell him the truth. Misty had said it had been disgusting when she first got there, spending hours cleaning the place up. He didn't need to know the truth. Just like he didn't need to know how slutty his daughter was.

"Still beautiful and in one piece. The views were spectacular."

"Yeah, those views were something else," William added.

"How long has it been since we've been up here?" Her dad's question surprised her mom who was still rambling on about some café they'd found overlooking the beach.

"How on Earth would I know?" Amber's stepmom snapped.

Amber's dad turned his attention to her, "Well, I'm going to unpack and check my messages. You two stay out of trouble."

Amber watched him leave as William turned on some music, a bass-thumping disco-tech style. He grabbed Amber's hand and pulled her up the pair of them dancing. It was the only thing that finally made the negativity go away. Clapping her hands out of time with the beat, she moved her body. She didn't care. Amber was letting herself find the beat, losing herself to the music. The beats were her lover as she and William danced together.

"You ready to head out to the club?"

"Oh, you're leaving already?" her stepmom feigned being upset.

"I promised him we'd go," Amber replied, hoping she wouldn't ask to tag along.

"Well, be careful, dear." Her stepmom gave her a quick wave as she and William headed out.

*****

The cab dropped them off in front of a club that was pulsing with light and sound. It rattled her chest and she loved it. They danced and drank, and she didn't think about Jack once.

"Looking good, sister."

"Looking pervy, brother."

They laughed and order a few more drinks, taking a seat, both of them sweaty from dancing so much.

"Oh, I think we have a potential suitor for you to bed, my darling," William drawled, showing Amber his phone.

There was something darkly erotic about her brother picking the men for her to fuck. It was wrong. It was dirty. But she didn't care.

It didn't take her long to realize that there weren't a whole lot of potential guys. She flicked her finger across the screen as she went through the pictures. They were all a little too European for her tastes, but she wasn't going to be picky at the moment.

"This was such a good idea."

"I'm glad you thought so. I'll take complete credit."

"I knew you would."

Finishing her wine, she smiled at him. "I was thinking about taking a trip. You know, just to clear my head, maybe push the reset button."

"I need one of those."

"You need so much more than just that," she said playfully.

"Ouch. I never knew you to be so snarky about my needs."

"Well, now you know."

William finished his drink and said, "We should probably get going. Probably not that hard to get a cab this time of night."

She had no idea what time it was and didn't care. Amber was having a good time and loving every minute of it with William. She warpped an arm around him and hugged him and then kissed his cheek. William fanned himself with his open hand like a shy schoolboy. "Oh, my."

"Perv."

"You know it, girl. Come on, let's get going."

They got up from their table, another couple swooping in to take it, the room still crowded, the dance floor hopping. She hadn't realized how much she'd missed going out with William and just letting loose.

As they leave the club and stepped down to the sidewalk, William hugged her and said, "You should wear that more often."

"What? This dress? Are you kidding me? I hate this dress."

"No, not the dress, dumbass. That smile. You look good when you smile."

"Yeah, I've been kind of a mess lately. But you've helped me tonight, William. You really have."

"Well, I hope you remember this night when I ask you for a favor sometime in the near future."

"You're extorting favors from me?" She reached for him to give him another hug when someone grabbed her roughly from behind and jerked her away from William.

Almost falling, she stumbled and twisted her ankle, her hands swinging wildly at her attacker. Punching him twice in the face, the man grabbed her wrists and growled at her. His eyes were golden, canines extended.

"Jack?" she gasped, her eyes wide with shock.

She knew he was going to change. She could see it in his eyes.

She also realized William was sprawled out on the sidewalk moaning. What had Jack done to him? Was he all right?

As he started to sit up, William said, "Get away from her, you asshole."

Jack growled and snarled at him. "Amber is mine. I claim her as mine."

William tried to stand and fell back to the ground. He tried to right himself one more time and was successful at regaining his feet.

"Stand down, or pay the price," Jack growled.

Raising his hands in a submissive sign, William backed away from them both averting his eyes as a show of respect.

Amber couldn't believe what was happening. Anger boiling over, she slapped Jack over and over, trying to get away from him. She wasn't sure what he was capable of, but frightened about what he had just done. Amber kept trying to wrench her arm free, but Jack's grip was like a vice. He wasn't letting go. What had him so angry?

19

Jack

How could she do this? Throwing herself at this guy? And hugging on the other guys in the bar? He wanted to fuck her and mark her, claiming her as his mate.

Yanking her down the alleyway along the side of the club, they could feel the pulsing music from inside through the vibrations of the alley wall. A single streetlight at the end kept them hidden in the shadows. Shoving her against the wall, he used his body weight to hold her in place, kissing her roughly. He was surprised when she pushed back, her arms around him, pulling him closer.

"You do know that was my brother, right? My *very* gay brother," she said when he broke away from their kiss.

He didn't care. He silenced her with another rough kiss, his hand in her hair, holding her still. Kissing wildly, they caressed each other, Amber extending her panther claws to pierce his back, the needling pain exciting him further. He growled, his desire leaking out of his hardened member that was feeling constricted in the confines of his trousers. He had to take her and take her now. His panther was urging him to claim her as their mate.

Tugging her dress down, he could hear the noise of the people walking along the sidewalk at the end of the alley. He hoped they could see her beautiful body and know they couldn't have her. He had never wanted another woman as much as he wanted Amber right now. Jack wanted to take her roughly, let the passersby hear her moan when he made her come hard. He wanted them to know he owned her and she owned him.

He groaned against her as they kissed roughly again, their mouths fighting each other for dominance. Jack rubbed himself against her wetness, both still partially clothed, Amber moaning. He tugged her dress even more, exposing her breasts to the watchful eyes of anyone who wanted to see her. It enthralled him even more, his member throbbing with so much desire. He needed to claim her and mark her as his.

Unzipping his pants, he freed his erection and forced it beneath her skirt. One thrust and he was fully inside her, sheathing himself. Wrapping her legs around his waist, she drew him closer urging him deeper.

"Yes," she panted. "Fuck me hard."

He thrusted his hips, rutting hard, her hips rocked along with his rhythm. They bucked together, meeting each other's thrusts. Faster and faster, they went until they both cried out as they came together. It was quick and powerful, neither wanted it to end. He didn't want to stop. He hadn't marked her yet.

"Hey what are they doing down there?" a voice shouted from the end of the alleyway.

He turned to look down the alley, Amber following his gaze, and put on a show for them. She turned so they could see her bare breasts, Jack thrusting even harder. They both came again, their urgency making them both tremble.

"I want to mark you but I can't, not here," Jack panted.

"Why not? I think they like the show."

"I love showing you off to them and wouldn't mind letting them get a closer look."

He still moved in and out of her, but it was in slow movements.

"Baby, did you hear me when I said I needed to mark you?"

"You mean?"

Jack nodded. "You're mine. You have me so hard, I don't want to stop fucking you."

"Oh, Jack. God, yes. Please give it to me. Please, don't make me wait any longer."

He pumped his hips over and over, Amber getting louder and louder with each thrust until he exploded inside her again, pumping her full just like she'd wanted and just like he needed. He loved the idea of her being full of his seed and could picture her having his cub.

"Marking you has to just be the two of us."

Amber nodded, kissing him. "Then let's find somewhere else to be."

He broke their kiss to look at her. He needed to see her face when he told her. Her reaction. "If I mark you, we are together forever. You are mine. You can't leave again, okay?"

Narrowing her eyes at him, he asked, "What's wrong?"

"I caught you kissing Trina in your office. That's why I left."

He closed his eyes, still inside her. "She caught me off guard. I didn't know she was going to do that. Baby, we didn't do anything. I made her leave."

"You're not lying to me, are you?" Her claws raked across his back, the pain a bright flash. One that was triggering him to shift and mark her already.

His nostrils flared. "No, of course not. You're the one I want Amber. You're my mate. I want you to be my partner forever. How does that sound?"

Her smile faltered and he was worried she was going to say no but she surprised him by saying, "I've been trying to fight it but I can't. That's why I went out on some dates but nothing worked. It was all wrong."

"What was wrong?"

"None of them were you."

They kissed again, their bodies keeping the rhythm going. When they finally broke the kiss, Jack said, "I'm sorry I scared your brother."

"It's okay. He deserves a good scare now and then."

Chuckling he said, "My panther wants to come out and mate with yours."

She moaned and bit her lower lip for a moment. "I know a place where we can go."

20

Amber

They were all over each other in the car on the way to her place. She was oozing from Jack's seed and loved her legs were slick with it. Amber couldn't wait to get him inside the guesthouse where she lived behind her parent's house. She needed to feel him inside her again. She was ready to claim him as her mate as well.

"How did you find me?" she asked.

Jack turned onto her street, smiling. "Your mom told me."

"Stepmom."

He raised his fingers from the steering wheel. "Sorry. I just explained to her how important it was for me to find you and she helped out."

"Just like her to meddle in my affairs."

"Are you sorry she told me?"

Reaching across the seat, she gripped his member still hard in his pants, and he gasped as she said, "No, why are you?"

"Not at all. I'm sorry things went so wrong. And I'm sorry about Trina. I should've said something to you."

Pulling to the curb, he put the car in park and asked, "Is there anything I can do to make it up to you?"

Undoing her seatbelt, she leaned across and unzipped his pants, freeing his member and taking him in her mouth.

Moving her mouth along the shaft, she teased the tip, his body shuddering with pleasure. She smiled around his erection. He trembled again and she worked a little faster.

"Amber."

Her name was just a husky whisper in the car, and she loved it, forcing his length fully into her mouth. She didn't stop there, nibbling at the base. He filled her mouth, pulsing three times in quick succession. She swallowed it all.

Sitting up, his thickness still in her hand, she kissed him gently on the mouth before looking at him seductively and whispered, "Let's go inside my place."

"You might kill me before this night is over." He laughed, taking a deep breath as he got out of the car.

"Don't die on me yet."

"Oh, I don't think you'll have to worry about that just yet. My inner panther is dying to mate with yours, Amber. My legs are shaking, my heart pounding and all I can think about is being inside you again and mating with you. Making you truly mine by marking you."

"You can mark me in any way, you want. I'm yours, body and soul. I want to be used by you in every way. Please, I am your mate and you are mine, too."

She took his hand and led him around the side of the house to where she lived. The guest house was a cute stone cottage complete with a tile roof and stone walkway. Pushing through the gate, Jack squeezed her butt playfully and she giggled. God, she couldn't wait for him to be inside her again.

With the lights off, they stumbled into her cottage and back to the bedroom. Undressing each other with every step, his fingers found her wetness and he moaned.

"That's from me?"

"From both of us, but yes, you."

They quickly undressed and fell to the bed, his mouth finding her throat, before teasing the skin in a hot line to her bare breast. His lips and tongue teased her hardened nipples, her body arching from the sensation.

She loved his mouth, his scent, his urgency.

This time, he was a little more patient, his mouth teasing her to ecstasy, her body thrumming with pleasure. Little blossoms of desire peppered her mind, as his mouth moved across her bare midriff. As his tongue swirled between her legs, she gripped a handful of hair as gently as she could, pushing her hips to meet his mouth.

"God, Jack. I'm right there."

And then, she was.

The orgasm rocked her, body trembling, his mouth kissing, licking, teasing. Looking at her, she smiled. She'd never felt this way before when any man. Jack was insatiable and he was hers.

Moving up along her body, his bare skin felt so hot against hers. Parting her legs, he slid inside her, and they both moaned. Staring into each other's eyes, they smiled, their breath coming faster.

As their pace increased, his thrusts growing stronger, she knew she wanted to be with him always. There had never been a man to make her feel what she was drowning in right now. It was love. Pure love.

Her inner panther felt that wonderful bloom of love and desire. "Make me yours."

And he did.

As he arched his back and plunged deeper inside her, hips meeting hips, mouths finding mouths, they climbed and climbed until, their pleasure spilled over, both orgasming at the same time. He sank his teeth into the base of her neck, marking her, tasting her sweat, and her passion. They shuddered and held each other, their breath finally slowing down a bit, his member still inside her.

The light breaking through the parted curtains spilled across them in white lines, the moon overhead almost full. She could see the goosebumps scattering across his skin, occasionally, in a blanket of motion.

Pulling out, he nuzzled next to her, their legs entwined, each of them finally sated, finally happy, finally content.

"I've never felt anything close to this," Jack mumbled against her throat as he kissed her.

"Me neither."

"What do you think it means?"

"That we're probably dreaming." She giggled softly.

"I hope not."

"If we are, I hope it goes on forever. I don't ever want to wake up if this is a dream."

"Me neither."

The words didn't feel unnatural. Nothing was fake. Nothing was put on. There was no saying what the other person wanted to hear. Amber felt completely different than she usually did with Jack. She'd said similar things to countless men before in her life because she thought that's what was expected. It was that way in the movies and all the romance novels she'd read when she was young. But this, this was different. She hadn't felt those things or even loved the men she'd been with even when she'd said the words.

"What are you thinking?"

"What makes you think I was thinking?"

"You get this cute little crease between your eyes above your nose when you are thinking. It's sweet. Cute."

"Shut up. Really?"

Jack nodded, his fingers tracing a circle around her nipple, making her giggle. She was ticklish there and didn't know it. Even more so to his touch. She smiled. Feeling an odd sense of contentment like she'd never felt.

"Nobody's ever told me that before."

He smiled at her, kissing her shoulder. His eyes almost looked silver in the moonlight; his muscular body molded against hers. Arm behind his head, she toyed with his hair, a bit curlier than usual with all the activity in the past hour.

"So, are you going to let me in on the secret?"

"What secret?"

"Whatever you were thinking about."

"Oh, that." She bit her tongue.

"Yes, that."

She shrugged, fingers still moving through his hair, the feel of his body comforting and arousing at the same time. "I'm not sure I was thinking anything specific. I've just never been so completely happy. I mean, the sex was great, but I've had great sex before."

"Ouch."

"Stop. What I mean is sex can feel great with just about anyone. It's mostly mental, right? But what we just had, was more than just great sex. It was like we were connected physically and spiritually."

"That's mating. Being marked."

"It's fantastic. Have you marked any others?"

Jack shook his head side to side, his stubble tickling her bare skin. "No. I've never found anyone I genuinely wanted to be with you. This is a first for me too. What about you? Have you been close?"

Nodding, she felt the emotion of the moment, tears suddenly welling in her eyes. Jack noticed right away, sitting up and drawing her to him.

"Did I say something wrong?"

"No, not at all. Everything's fine. I was just thinking, that's all."

"Ah-ha! You *were* thinking!" He pointed a finger at her with an amused look on his face before kissing her.

"It's just something that happened in college. It's silly I guess." Her smile faltered the emotion back in a thick current.

"Nothing's silly. Not tonight. Not ever. Tell me about it."

"I was close one time. I mean, I thought I was. We dated for over two years while in college and even moved in together. It was all so new and wonderful. I could see myself having kids with him, growing old together. We had a great sex life and were picking out curtains together and flooring and stuff I never imagined that could be so much fun.

She grew quiet, Jack gently caressing her bare side. "What happened?"

"I came home early from class one night. We didn't have much money at the time so it was a big deal to eat out. Well, I wanted to surprise him by taking him out to dinner only he wasn't the one who was surprised."

"What do you mean?"

"I caught him in bed with another girl. I just stood there in the doorway watching. I counted the thuds of my heart as it broke. One, the girl looked at my reflection in the mirror, our eyes meeting, as he mounted her from behind. He didn't even see me at first. The look on the girl's face wasn't horror at being caught or even surprise. It was one of amusement. I wanted to just kill her. And him."

"I'm so sorry."

"Oh, I'm not done yet."

"Oh, no."

"Oh, yeah. So, he finally noticed me in the mirror and he doesn't pull out. He just keeps plowing away, smiling at me. Smiling at me while his dick was in another woman. What an asshole."

"Grade-A."

"I had asked how he could do such a thing and I swear I think the girl was coming while I was asking him. Anyway, he said to me that he didn't understand why I was so upset that it was fun and all but it was time to part ways."

"Part ways?"

"Yeah."

"Who says that?"

"Assholes apparently."

They were quiet a moment before Jack sighed. "You know you're not that girl anymore. You're not in college. And I'm not that asshole."

She giggled, "I know. It just hit me."

"Are you still looking?"

"I don't need to."

"Why?"

"I have everything I've ever wanted right here with you."

They stayed in bed, the moment lingering, the love blossoming. She'd never felt so content. As they kissed softly, his stomach growled.

"Hungry?"

"Yeah, I didn't get a chance to eat. I was too busy stalking you and beating up your brother," Jack laughed softly.

"Oh, that's right. I can whip us up something if you like."

"How about just a sandwich. I don't think I can handle anything heavy right now. Liable to shower you in puke."

"See, right there. That's one reason I love you so much."

He chuckled. "Why?"

"Because even when you talk about puke, it's romantic."

Kissing each other, she got up and made them sandwiches. Who knew peanut butter and jelly sandwiches could be so romantic? She loved it.

"This is the finest peanut butter and jelly sandwich I've ever had."

"Oh, stop."

"I've never been paid for sex with food before," Jack said jokingly.

"You're so bad." She playfully slapped his arm before devouring half her sandwich. She hadn't realized how much of an appetite she had worked up.

As they finished, she had an idea. "Are you up for a run?"

His smile was devilish. "I could probably be convinced."

"Then let's go."

*****

Twenty minutes later, they pulled into a large nature preserve. It was in the early hours in the morning, the sun was due to rise in a few hours. It was the perfect time to be out and shift. Getting out of the car, they went to the rear of the SUV. Popping the hatch, they undressed. Neither one of them could stop smiling, Amber overwhelmed with what she felt in her heart.

A moment later, the pair were naked, holding hands and gazing into the darkening woods.

"Are you ready?" he asked her.

"If you're with me, yes."

Jack kissed her, their bodies close, their lips lingering for a moment. And then, the pair launched themselves into the darkness, their panthers escaping their human bounds. Sated and satisfied, they moved as a pair through the woods.

Amber knew where she wanted to take him and veered off to the right. The moonlight glanced off her body, lithe, darting between the trees. She could hear him moving alongside her, the pair breaking into a clearing, the moon's light taking the color away, the black and white movie of them slowing and nuzzling each other played out.

As things got more physical, the nuzzling became more aggressive, the feel of his fur against hers was incredible, she turned and remained on all fours, showing herself to him. He didn't wait, mounting her, extending his claws as he held on to her haunches.

She mewled to him, as he thrust inside her roughly. His hips flexing against her, driving his engorged thickness deeper. He was hitting that sweet spot she loved so much, feeling his rhythm. His claws dug in a little deeper and she shivered, the pleasure building.

He nibbled across the back of her neck and she came all over him. He orgasmed a moment later, shuddering as he collapsed across her back. Slipping out of her, they curled up together in the grass a moment, relishing the mating ritual, bathed in moonlight.

They stretched and she shimmered as she changed back into her human form, Jack following suit a moment later. He curled his hand at the small of her back drawing her to him. Kissing his lips, she spread her legs, the wetness dripping out of her. Panthers sated, she straddled him and took his swollen member inside her. Riding him, the night alive around her with sounds and smells, the moon turning her skin almost translucent.

"Amber, you feel so incredible."

She moaned, grinding her hips as she continued to ride him. "God, yes. This feels amazing."

Their passion grew, Jack swelling inside her, so thick and firm. She couldn't stop herself. "I'm there, baby," she moaned.

"Yes. Please don't stop riding me," he groaned, and she knew he was close. "I'm ready to fill you up again."

"Yes." Her hands rubbed his chest, her hair wild around her face. It was perfect. She hoped someone was watching them. The idea of someone seeing something so wonderfully sacred was heaven. She loved Jack. She loved him for all that he had given her and for all the life they had yet to live. They came together, eyes looking at each other, never once looking away as the pulsing pleasure took them over that edge again and again.

21

Jack

He couldn't stop smiling. The fact Amber had accepted him was incredible to him. Especially after her not talking to him for so long. She was his mate. His partner. His one true person. They held hands on the way back to her cottage. He wanted to take her home to formally introduce her to his mom.

"Would you do that with me?" he asked her.

"I would love to but I can't just yet. I need to let my father know. He's the pack alpha's third and their lawyer. I'd like to tell my parents first if that's okay."

"It's more than okay. I love it. When do you want to introduce me?" Jack felt like a school kid who just won the homecoming game and had just been crowned the king, dancing with his queen. He was walking on air and had no intention of coming down anytime soon.

"Today, but we need to get cleaned up first."

They took a shower together to wash off the delicious scent of sex from them. He was thankful for that. Nothing worse than being introduced to the father of your lover smelling like her. He chuckled as the water cascaded down over them both. The steam clouded the shower door, the two of them reduced to water blurs of motion.

"I can't believe this."

"You better start," Jack said, kissing her deeply.

The soap and shampoo scent swept him away, her hair wet against her scalp, spilling over her shoulder, like a question mark.

They took their time washing each other's backs, kisses and caresses abound, the steam making it all seem surreal. He loved every moment and was reluctant to get out even when the hot water started to turn cold.

Toweling off, they dressed and headed to the main house to meet her parents. He wasn't overly nervous about it. He knew it was a formality. He was excited to make it official so the pack and world knew they were together.

*****

"He's in the study," Amber said and directed him down a hallway.

He recognized Alan. They'd met a few years ago when he'd come to the Wyoming cabin. He had seemed nice, intelligent, and a loving family person.

Alan pulled his glasses down as Amber said, "Dad, this is Jack. Jack this is my dad, Alan."

"Sir, how are you?" Jack extended his hand, her dad accepting with a curious look.

"I wanted you to meet him. We've mated and accepted each other."

"I'm very well, thank you. It's been a while. What was that four, five years ago up at the cabin?"

The look of shock wasn't lost on him as Amber's jaw dropped looking between the two of them.

"Wait, you've already met?"

Jack chuckled, Alan joining him as they broke their handshake.

"We met when I went to Deerskin Peaks on one of my trips. I just needed a break from the city. Needed to decompress and you definitely do that there."

"Yes, you can," Jack said.

"So, you've chosen her as your mate?"

"Yes, sir. She's beautiful and smart. I think we are matched perfectly."

Alan nodded and sniffed, smiling at Amber. "I'm excited for you both. It's about time you found your mate, young lady.

"Dad." Amber seemed a little embarrassed and a little put out by Alan's comments.

"Jack, no worries about the union. I fully accept and can't wait to see what the future brings. I've been trying to match her with a mate for some time now and I'm glad to see it finally happening, especially with someone like you."

Jack's heart swell with happiness at receiving Alan's blessing. He smiled at Amber who was watching him with a curious expression. She was glowing and he could sense her happiness. It was genuine and it made him feel elated. He had finally found his mate.

22

Amber

One Year Later

Amber still felt like she was walking on clouds every time she thought about the blessings she had in her life. Living with Jack was one. The passion and love they held for each other only continued to grow stronger. Her parents were happy for them both was a huge one. Her father was truly overjoyed by the prospect of her and Jack being together. The fact he was a werepanther and an alpha to boot was a bonus. The other bonus was he already knew Jack and that they got along really well.

Jack honked the horn of his truck. She drew back the living room curtain of the house she had moved in with Jack and waved to him. He motioned for her to come outside while he stayed in the driver's seat.

What was he up to?

She smiled walking up along the driver's side, his window down.

"Hey sailor, care to show me your submarine? Maybe I can suck on your periscope," she waggled her eyebrows.

"Nice," he said with a laugh. Amber knew that Jack was still glad that her naughty sense of humor hadn't changed.

"What's up?"

"I was wondering if someone might not like to accompany someone else to a special dinner. It's been a year since we met." He reached for her hand, but she ignored it and stood on her tiptoes to kiss him instead.

"I'd love to," she said against his lips. She still had an insatiable appetite for him, and he still sated her hunger, but tonight, he seemed to be on a mission.

"Hop in."

She thought about going back inside to change out of her jeans and sweater but decided to say screw it. She was with Jack. She didn't care how she looked to anyone. She only cared about the look on his face every time he looked at her. Amber never knew it was so easy to see love on someone else's face. It was breathtaking.

As they pulled away from the curb, she took his hand in hers.

"I know it's not New York City, but I wanted it to be nice."

"I'm sure it'll be wonderful," she said cheerfully. "Where are you taking me?"

"It's a surprise."

"Well, then I have a surprise for you too."

"What? Are you taking me to dinner tomorrow night?"

"No, but you are going to have to start making reservations for three soon."

"For three? Does your dad want…" He didn't finish the sentence, his eyes filling with tears. He figured it out. "Are you serious?"

She nodded, squeezing his hand. "Yes. Due in the spring."

"Are you serious?"

Her eyebrows knitted in confusion. "Yes. Do you not believe me?"

He laughed. It was such a good laugh. "I think we can reschedule this," he said, turning the truck around. "I need to take you back home and straight to bed and make love to you all night long."

Amber's face hurt from smiling so much. Her head was swimming with joyful thoughts and her heart was swelled with glee, thinking about the wonderful life they were going to have together now that they were expanding their family. After helping Misty deliver her twins, she knew then that someday she wanted to have a family of her own. It was such a wonderful experience to be there to see life coming into the world.

Amber couldn't wait to tell Misty and her family. She'd never felt such love from another human being before Jack. She looked at Jack and he at her. Neither one of them could stop smiling, enjoying each moment as it came, together.

Epilogue

Jack

Jack couldn't believe how happy he was. Amber seemed to get more beautiful every day. He wasn't sure if it was because she was pregnant or if it was their love growing so strongly every day. Whatever the reason, he simply couldn't stop smiling at her, always kissing and touching, experiencing an intimacy that he had never known. He had never been with another woman where he wanted to be with her all the time. Jack figured she must be meant to be his mate if he felt that strongly about her.

They had let her parents know what was going on and they were thrilled with the news. His mom had already started talking about plans for the baby and where they would live. He wasn't sweating any of those decisions. Surprisingly, he was calmer than he had ever been.

Amber came out of the kitchen and into the living room where he sat and hugged him, his mom in tow, and members of his small pack visited, bringing gifts for the expected child.

"How are you feeling?" Amber asked, hugging him tightly. She was starting to show a lot more and it thrilled him to no end.

"I'm a little afraid to say."

She squeezed his hand and shook it a bit. "What's that supposed to mean?"

Each member of the pack set down gifts on the table just inside the door and walked toward them as they sat in the living room. His chest swelled as each one greeted them cheerfully.

"If this is a dream and I wake up tomorrow without you, I'm not sure I'd make it."

"That's not going to happen. I'm here. I'm not going anywhere."

"I know. Amber, I love you so much."

"Love you too, Jack."

As the pack congratulated them, they began to talk and laugh together about how a new life in the pack was a wonderful blessing. Jack never let go of Amber's hand. He had to keep the dream alive. And when he thought he was being silly, he'd look at Amber and realize he was willing to take that chance of looking silly if it meant he could hold onto the wonderful dream Amber had given to him.

About J. Raven Wilde

J. Raven had spent most of her life traveling around the US or abroad, managing to find a bookstore in every city she visited. She began writing when she was a little girl, and it slowly grew into something she loved doing.

Now that she isn't traveling as much anymore, she spends her time writing steamy romance stories at her quiet modest home by the lake.

Connect with J. Raven Wilde

If you loved this story, sign up to receive J. Raven's newsletter at www.TwistedCrowPress.com. Subscribers get the latest information on cover reveals, new or upcoming releases, and promos. Plus, it's FREE, and she promises never to spam you or give out your information. You can also follow her on her Facebook Group, Wilde Raven's Steamy Reads.

Printed in Great Britain
by Amazon